LA ROSA DE MATANZAS

(THE ROSE OF MATANZAS)

MILTON J. DAVIS

MVmedia, LLC
Fayetteville GA

Milton J. Davis/MVmedia, LLC
PO Box 1465
Fayetteville, GA 30214
www.mvmediaatl.com

Publisher's Note: This is a work of fiction. Names, characters, places, and incidents are a product of the author's imagination. Locales and public names are sometimes used for atmospheric purposes. Any resemblance to actual people, living or dead, or to businesses, companies, events, institutions, or locales is completely coincidental.

Book Layout ©2017BookDesignTemplates.com
Cover Art by Marcellus Shane Jackson
Cover Design by Kecia Stovall

Ordering Information:
Quantity sales. Special discounts are available on quantity purchases by corporations, associations, and others. For details, contact the "Special Sales Department" at the address above.

La Rosa De Matanzas/ Milton J. Davis. -- 1st ed.
ISBN 978-0-9992789-9-4

Contents

Dedicated to Antonio Maceo, the Bronze Titan

'Un Hombre como tal, jamás tiene que ser olvidado."

- 1 -

Hernando Gomez squinted as he studied the narrow path just beyond the palm trees. The tropical sun illuminated the roadway, making it dangerous for those seeking to remain hidden, those like Gomez. Common sense told him to stick to the bush, but time was of the essence. He and his men were far beyond their territory and had most likely been detected so it was essential that they accomplish their task in earnest.

He removed his straw hat then wiped the sweat from his forehead before turning to look into the stern face of his companion. The man's tan complexion contrasted with Gomez's umber hue. Both men were dressed similar, but other man's mannerisms revealed his true origins. He was Freedonian.

"What do you think?" the man said in stilted Spanish.

"I don't think it's wise to take the trail, señor," Hernando said.

"We haven't encountered anyone else for three days," the man replied. "I think it's safe to say we are the only ones in the area."

Hernando frowned. "We will stay off the trail."

The man sucked his teeth. "I don't think . . ."

"Pardon me señor, you hired me because of my expertise," Hernando said. "If I say we stay in the bush, we stay in the bush. That is unless you have decided to hire someone else."

The man studied Hernando for a moment before answering.

"We'll do as you say," he answered.

Hernando and the man worked their way deeper into the bush. The more time he spent with these foreigners, the less he liked them. It didn't matter that they were Freedonians or that they supplied his men with guns and provisions. They had no business in Cuba.

But then again, who was he to complain? He was a bandit playing at being rebel, a man whose loyalty was for sale to the highest bidder. The anemic revolt that plagued the eastern half of Cuba known as Oriente was not his concern. It was a rich man's war; wealthy plantation owners attempting to shrug the imperial yoke of New Spain for their own benefit. People like him would not profit from it; they would still answer and serve those who they served now. It was then he remembered why he helped the Freedonians. They promised a freedom where all would prosper. He would be able to give up his nefarious ways, open a shop in Havana, and maybe even get married.

The quiet was shattered by the shrill cry of a startled macaw.

"Get down!" Hernando shouted.

Gatling gun fire drowned out the hapless bird, bullets ripping through the trees. Hernando and the Freedonian crawled toward the others as urgent voices mingled with the rapid gunfire.

"Alto! Alto!"

The ground vibrated as trees snapped behind them. Hernando took a quick look then grimaced; two Diablos crashed through the thicket, their exposed drivers searching for the bandits with telescopic goggles. The metal tracks crushed the palmettos and small pines in their paths as the mechanical behemoths spewed thick steam clouds from the exhaust pipes rising from the rear of the vehicles. Hernado's men were already fleeing when Hernando and the Freedonian reached them. The other Freedonians crouched behind cover, their faces stern. Bulky leather bags were strapped to their backs, the contents unknown. Each carried a shotgun and a machete.

"I don't understand," the Freedonian shouted. "How did they know?"

"We can discuss that later, señor," Hernando said. "Now we must go."

"Down!" one of the Freedonians yelled.

Hernado dove to the ground as another round of bullets shredded the surrounding vegetation. The shooting paused long enough for Hernado and the Freedonian to scramble to their feet and hide behind a thick pine.

"I have a mission," the Freedonian said, his face resolved. "We're not going anywhere."

"You can stay and fight those things if you like," Hernando said. "I was paid to guide you. I wasn't paid to fight for you."

The firing ceased, replaced by cursing and shouting. The Freedonian looked at Hernando, then to the Diablos A thick stand of pines and palms blocked their path The Freedonian grinned like a lucky gambler.

"We'll go," he said. "But not before saying goodbye. Boys?"

The Freedonians took off the mysterious back packs then opened them. They extracted metal tubes which they quickly assembled. The third man took off his back pack and opened it, revealing four large bullet shaped objects which he carefully handled. The other men lifted the assembled tubes onto their shoulders. Hernando noticed a sight on the right side the tubes.

The Diablos continued to struggle with the brush, their automatic guns silent.

"Do you have a good shot?" the Freedonian said to his tube bearing men.

Both nodded.

"Good. Load them up, Travis. Let's see what these Diablos can handle."

Travis inserted the large bullet-like objects into the tubes, patting each man on the shoulder when done. The Freedonian and Travis hurried away from tube bearers, and then covered their ears. Hernando did the same.

The men jerked as a plume of smoke shot from behind and before their tubes, a sound like an on-coming train filled the thicket. Moments later both Diablos exploded, each one careening in different directions. The tube bearing Freedonians looked at the other man then gave him thumbs up. The Freedonian grinned.

"Now we go," he said.

The Freedonians packed up their weapons then fled in the direction of Hernando's men. Hernando hesitated, watching the sinister vehicles burn and spew black smoke. A smile came to his face. Maybe these Freedonians were useful after all.

* * *

The ebony hued man in the tailored white linen suit sat in the open-air cabana, twirling a cigar between his long fingers. He took out his pocket watch, frowning as he checked the time. His man was late, which wasn't like him. It was possible that his mission had been compromised and he lay dead in some unknown place, but the man in the suit had to be sure. He'd wait another fifteen minutes then be on his way.

John Scobel didn't normally take on field assignments. As head of the Freedonian Dispatch, the department responsible for Freedonia security and intelligence, he reported directly to Vice President Tubman and was the final say for any and all operations. His field days should have been long behind him, but some operations were important enough for his personal attention. The Cuban operations fell into that category. To those in Havana, he was a Freedonian tobacco merchant, waiting to meet a local farmer to discuss his current crop. His purpose was far more serious.

His man entered the cabana as he looked up. The look on his face told him everything he needed to know.

"That bad?" John asked.

The man pulled out a chair from the small table then slumped into it.

"Yes," he answered. "I think we got closer this time, but they were waiting."

"A traitor within the ranks?"

A waiter came to their table, tall and pale-skinned with black hair plastered to his head with pomade and sweat.

"Welcome señor. What would you like?"

"A mojito," the man replied.

The waiter nodded then hurried away.

"Most likely," the man continued. "The resistance is disorganized. On the one hand, you have the plantation owners fighting for more control of the island and higher political status. On the other hand, you have the workers fighting for freedom and representation. Neither trusts each other, so there's little hope for unification."

John chewed on his cigar. "And meanwhile New Spain continues its plans. What about the merchandise?"

The man grinned. "The only bright spot. It performed very well."

The waiter returned with the man's drink.

"*Gracias,*" he said.

"*De nada,*" the waiter replied.

The man took a long swig, and then wiped his mouth with his sleeve.

"There is one thing, though," he said. "Apparently it hasn't always been this way. Ten years ago, the rebels were united. They were on the verge of defeating New Spain before their alliance collapsed."

John leaned closer to the man. "What happened?"

"There was a meeting planned for the final operation. Somehow it was discovered. Most of the leaders were either killed or captured. A few escaped. Some say they fled to South America, probably Brazil. Soon afterwards the plantation owners accepted New Spain's surrender terms."

"Those who escaped; do you know who they are?"

The man nodded. He reached into his shirt pocket then extracted a folded piece of paper. John took it then opened it. There were three names on the list; one name underlined and circled.

"Two of them are beyond our reach," the man said. "Any questions about them would raise suspicions. The one whose name is circled is another matter."

"Paulina de Rosa," John said, reading the name aloud. "Who is she?"

"She's one of the organizers of the first revolutionary coalition," the man said. "It's believed she was the person that brought the planters into the conflict."

"Is she alive or dead?"

"Alive."

John folded the paper then put it in his pocket.

"Any idea where she's hiding?"

The man smiled then finished his mojito.

"Freedonia."

- 2 -

Pauline emerged from the feed shed and saw a sight that made her laugh until she cried. Feed spilled from the tilted bucket in her left hand and the chickens swarmed about her legs, helping themselves to the unexpected bounty. She wiped her eyes, and then pressed her hand against her chest to stop the laughter. The source of her humor cursed as he struggled with plow and mule, cutting a ragged row in the mixture of rich black loam and red Georgia clay.

"Zeke Culpepper, you are a terrible farmer," Pauline said out loud.

She finished feeding the fowl, returned the feed bucket to the shed and then strolled to the field. Zeke's cursing grew louder as she approached.

"God damn beast from hell!" he shouted. "If you don't move your ass . . ."

"Wrong animal," Pauline called out.

Zeke snarled at Pauline and she laughed.

"How in the hell do you do this?" he asked.

Pauline walked up the roan mule's head then reached into her pocket. She took out a handful of feed and offered it to the beast. The mule ate it eagerly.

"Angelina ain't so bad," she said. "She's just . . . stubborn as a mule."

"You need a new one," Zeke snapped. "One that ain't so ornery."

"No, sir." Pauline patted Angelina hard on the neck. "This girl is a worker. She's keeps the same pace from sun up to sun down. She just gets a little fickle now and then. She bit you yet?"

Zeke's eyes went wide. "You knew she was going to do that?"

"Yep." Pauline sauntered to Zeke, and then unhooked the harness.

"You sure do cuss a lot for a deacon," she said.

Zeke patted her butt. "That and other things."

"Keep your mind on the right task," she said. "Angelina is just like every animal on this farm, including the two-legged one. You just need to let her know who's in charge."

She put on the plow harness, and then popped the reins.

"Hah!"

Angelina jumped into motion. Pauline walked behind her, steering her in a straight line. Zeke walked beside them.

"You should finish this field. You're doing such a good job."

"Oh no, mister," Pauline replied. "This is your farm. My fields are plowed. I'm just here to train and supervise."

"I should just hire some men," he said. "I have the money."

"And then what are you going to do?" Pauline asked.

"I'll find something," he replied.

Pauline reined Angelina to a halt. "You'll start bounty hunting again. "

Zeke looked away.

"No, I won't have it," she said.

"I'm not sure it's your place to say," Zeke replied. "It's not like you're Mrs. Culpepper."

Pauline smirked. She wasn't about to be led into that conversation.

She took off the harness then put it back on Zeke.

"Finish the field. Remember, be firm. Let her know who's boss."

Zeke gave Pauline a helpless look.

"Where are you going?"

"Into town. I need to pick up a few things." She walked toward the house.

"I can do it for you!" Zeke called out.

"I bet you could," Pauline called back.

"Take the automobile," Zeke shouted. "It's faster."

"I will," Pauline shouted back.

She went into the house to freshen up a bit before going into town, changing from her dirty coveralls to a narrow skirt and a short bodice suitable for driving. Going into town wasn't her favorite thing to do, but Zeke needed to practice and he would never get the hang of plowing with her around. It was hard breaking old habits, but being with Zeke made it easier, especially now that he'd given up bounty hunting. She didn't know where the money was coming from, but she honestly didn't care. As long as he was home, it was good.

She ambled out the back door to the automobile shed. The steam car sat in pristine condition, its emerald green body shining like a jewel. It was Zeke's pride and joy. It took her ages to get him to teach her how to the drive the machine, and a few more months before he let her drive solo. She went to the front, bending over to crank it to a start. The machine coughed to life, spewing steam from the tailpipe. She hurried to the barn door then opened it wide. Climbing in, she put on her goggles and hat then eased the car from the barn. The car chugged as she ran to close the shed then set out on her way, waving at Zeke as she sped by.

She jostled along the road to town, grinning as she thought of her good fortune. Who would have thought she would meet such a worldly man in such a small town? Sure, as capital of Freedonia Atlanta wasn't a backwater city. But compared to New York, Paris, or even Havana, the city had a long way to go when it came to sophistication. She shook her head; here she was reminiscing again. That life was over. It ended long before she and Angelo came to the young nation.

Thinking of Angelo saddened her. The sickness took him so fast she didn't have time to mourn him. He left everything he knew to be with her, even after she told him she didn't love him and probably never would. It didn't matter, he told her. He loved her and that was all that mattered.

"Angelo, Angelo," she whispered. "You were such a romantic."

She was so preoccupied she barely noticed the 'Welcome to Hapeville' sign. The town was the last stop before Atlanta, a market town for farmers unwilling to make the trip into the big city to sell their harvest. Pauline drove into town, spooking a few horses with the steam car. She parked near the Hapeville Hotel, took her basket from the passenger seat then strolled to the city market, waving at the shopkeepers and townsfolk along the way. She needed supplies, but her first destination was Miss Angie's flower cart. The jovial gray-haired lady waved as she approached, her ivory cheeks creased by her wide smile.

"Why, hello there, Miss Sunshine!" Pauline called out.

"Girl, if you were any brighter, we wouldn't need that ol' sun up there!" Miss Angie called back. The woman was dressed as brightly as her flowers, her yellow dress and bonnet adding flair to the otherwise drab market filled with dingy farmers.

The women hugged like mother and daughter.

"Come take a look at what I have today," Miss Angie said.

Pauline walked the length of the cart, making a show of inspecting each bloom.

"Your flowers are beautiful as always," Pauline said.

"A good bloom this year," Miss Angie said. "They all came up good and gorgeous."

"But none as beautiful as the roses, don't you think, Paulina?"

Pauline stiffened at the sound of the familiar voice, a voice she'd never hoped to hear again.

She turned to stare into the eyes of Philippe Gonzales. A thick moustache hid the Cuban officer's triumphant smile as he held out a red rose to her. She didn't recognize the men standing behind him, but it was no doubt they were Cuban regulars, their guns hidden inside their tweed jackets.

"Gonzales," Pauline said.

"*La Rosa*," Gonzales replied. "It's been a long time; a very long time."

"*¿Cómo me has encontrado?*" Pauline asked. The words felt rough in her mouth. It had been years since she spoke her native tongue.

"That is irrelevant." Gonzales dropped the rose, and then crushed it with his foot. Miss Angie began to protest, but Pauline shushed her.

"Where is Angelo?" he asked.

"He's dead."

Gonzales's eyes narrowed. "Don't lie to me, Paulina. The people in this town are very friendly. They say you live with a man who is not your husband. You have a farm a few miles away."

"I do live with a man, but it's not Angelo. As I said, he's dead."

"I will know soon enough. The rest of my men are on their way to your farm as we speak."

Pauline's stomach tightened. "Zeke's got nothing to do with this."

"Zeke is it? Then Zeke has nothing to fear," Gonzales answered. "You, however, are a different matter."

"Get it over with, then," she said.

"If only it was so easy," Gonzales replied. "If I had my way I would shoot you now, but the governor insists that I bring you back to Cuba to stand trial. There are still enough rebels alive that see you and the others as symbols and he wishes to end such notions once and for all. Saying you are dead is not as good as showing that you are."

"Pauline? What is going on?" Miss Angie asked.

Pauline turned to the old woman, and then forced a smile to her face.

"Everything is okay, Miss Angie. I have to go with these men. If you see Zeke, tell him I love him."

"No, everything is not okay!" Miss Angie shouted. She stepped into Gonzales's face. Pauline's heart raced as his men reached for their guns, but Gonzales waved them down.

"You're not going to get away with this!" Miss Angie said. "I'll go get the police!"

"*Senora*, I am only doing my duty for my country," Gonzales replied. "This woman is not who she appears to be. If you knew the crimes she has committed, you would not be so fond of her."

Miss Angie looked at Pauline, her expression revealing her confusion.

"Stay out of this Miss Angie. Please," Pauline urged.

She turned to Gonzales. "Let's go."

Gonzales took a pair of handcuffs from his jacket. Pauline extended her arms; she flinched as the handcuffs clicked around her wrists.

"*Gracias* for making this simple," Gonzales said. "We must hurry. There is a train waiting for us."

The two soldiers took position behind her as she followed Gonzales to the train station. Ten years she'd hid from them. Ten years.

"Goodbye, Zeke," she whispered. "I would have married you. I would have."

- 3 -

Zeke took a long drink from the ladle then dipped it into the well bucket for another sip. The field was plowed, more or less, and he was exhausted. Angelina wandered off to graze on a clump of grass near the fence, swishing her tail as if the day's work was of no consequence. Zeke studied the bite mark on his left hand, and then glared at the mule.

"If I didn't love Pauline so much . . ."

His statement fell short because of commotion in the distance. He stood then shaded his eyes with his hands. Five riders were coming fast, guns in hand. Zeke dropped the ladle then ran to the house. He leaped onto the porch, snatched open the screen door the hurried to his gun closet. He took out his leg holster, buckling it around his waist then grabbed his shotgun and jammed it in place. He then grabbed the Henri and as many bullets and shells he could shove in his pockets. By the time he slipped out the back door the men were riding up the road to his house.

Zeke leaned against the outside wall and then loaded both guns as the men galloped to the house. Whoever they were, they had no intentions of talking. They jumped off their horses, ran up the stairs then kicked in the door.

"Angelo! El juego ha terminado!"

The language made Zeke hesitate. Who in New Spain would have a grudge with him? It had been years since he'd served in the region and he hadn't been there long enough to make enemies. Worst of all, his name wasn't Angelo. Angelo was Pauline's brother and he was long dead. This had something to do with her.

The men ransacked the house. Zeke stayed low as he worked his way to the front of the house and the horses.

"Compruebe la parte posterior! Encuéntra-lo!"

Zeke opened the saddle bag of the nearest horse and then rummaged through it. The folded paper he discovered was familiar to a bounty hunt-er. What he saw on it shocked him. It was a picture of Pauline and Angelo.

"What the hell?"

He folded the wanted poster, and then stuck in into his shirt pocket.

"Alto!"

One of the riders stood at the door, his gun in his hand.

"You're standing in my house, buddy," Zeke said.

The man was fast, but Zeke was faster. He shot the intruder with the Henri, knocking him back into the house. Zeke ran around the outside as the other men shot at him through the walls and windows. The man blocking the back door was rais-ing his gun to fire when Zeke shot him. He charged inside then watched the other men running for their horses.

"I don't think so!" he hissed.

They were halfway down the road when Zeke came onto the porch. He took his time, adjusting the Henri's sight. Then he fired, shooting each man off his horse. Zeke looked about, making sure there was no one else before going to his barn then hitching his wagon. He collected the dead men's bodies, loaded them into the wagon, and then tied their horses to the wagon. This would be a slow ride, but he had to do things the right way. Inside his heart raced. These men were looking for Pauline. What the hell was going on?

He went straight to the constable's office when he arrived in Hapeville. Commander Jim Stall, a tall, wiry white man with thinning black hair and a gray beard met him as he climbed off the wagon. Commander Stall neared the wagon and spied Zeke's grim cargo. His friendly demeanor transformed to astonishment.

"Oh my God, Zeke! What have you done?"

"I didn't provoke this, Jimmy," Zeke answered. "The five of them rode up to my house while I was plowing the field. They kicked in the door and started tearing up the place. When I confronted them, they started shooting. I shot back."

He took the wanted poster from his shirt pocket then handed it to Stills.

"They had this on them."

The captain took the wanted poster. The look on his face told Zeke he'd seen it before. Stall refolded the poster then shoved it into his pants pocket.

"Is there something you need to tell me, Jimmy?" Zeke asked.

Stall looked about nervously before answering.

"Zeke, a man by the name of Philippe Gonzales came to my office a few days ago. He's a representative of the governor of Cuba. He had a warrant for Pauline's arrest. I didn't believe him at first. Miss Pauline has been an upstanding citizen. But when he presented me with the evidence, I had no choice but to stay out of his way. When Pauline came into town today, he took her into custody. I couldn't stop him, Zeke. Everything he had was official."

Zeke took off his cap then rubbed his head.

"So, Pauline's been arrested by the Cuban government?"

The captain nodded. "I'm afraid so."

Zeke went back to the wagon. He returned with his Henri.

"Where are they?"

Jimmy raised his hands. "Now hold on, Zeke. This ain't Oregon. This is an international situation. I'll have to report the deaths to the Freedonian authorities and they'll have to answer to New Spain. You will, too. Besides, they've already gone."

Zeke's eyes narrowed. "Where?"

Jimmy hesitated before answering. "They took the train to Savannah. I figure they'd catch a boat from there to Cuba."

Zeke walked away.

"Where are you going?" Joseph called out.

"To find my steamcar. Then I'm going home to pack."

The commander followed Zeke.

"Officially I must demand that you stay in the vicinity until the government authorities question you on this incident."

Zeke stopped then turned to face Jimmy.

"Do you plan on doing that, Jimmy? I really hope not."

Stall raised his hands.

"I don't want any trouble from you, Zeke. We've been friends too long and you're too good with that gun. Go on and do what you have to do. I can't help you if you're caught."

Zeke grinned. "I'll worry about that if it happens. Right now I got to go get Pauline."

"Pauline parked your car over by the hotel," Jimmy said.

"Thank you for the information," Zeke said.

Zeke left the wagon and the bodies with the commander. He was hurrying through the market when Miss Angie cut him off, holding a bouquet of daisies.

"They just took her, Zeke!" she said with watery eyes. "I tried to stop them but they took her!"

Zeke took the flowers, and then patted the woman's shoulder.

"Don't worry Miss Angie. I'm going to take her back."

Miss Angie tiptoed then kissed him on his cheek.

"You bring my baby back," she whispered. "And you kill those men. You got my permission."

"Yes ma'am," Zeke answered.

Zeke hesitated when he reached the automobile. Some of Pauline's items were still inside. Whoever took her was in a hurry. He set the flowers in the passenger seat then cranked the car to a start. He sped back to the farm, ignoring the bumps and dips he usually avoided. Once at the house he packed quickly, taking a few clothes, and a bag full of money. His destination wasn't Hapeville, it was Atlanta. He'd catch an airship to Savannah, which should put him in the harbor town before the train. Then he would wait. The next time he drove up to his farm, Pauline would be with him.

Zeke reached the Atlanta airship terminal by nightfall. As he rushed to the ticket booth, the ticket master was pulling the window gate closed.

"Wait!" he shouted.

"Sorry, we're closed for the day," the ticket master said. "Come back tomorrow."

"But I'm in a hurry! I need to leave tonight."

The ticket master frowned. "You know airships don't fly at night. At least not yet."

Zeke kicked the booth.

"Hey now!" the ticket master said. "No need to be destructive. Look, there's a nice little hotel about a mile from here. The owner runs a tight ship and the food is first rate. I'm sure she has a couple of rooms to spare tonight. She could use the money and you look like you need the rest."

The ticket master made sense. "Can I purchase a ticket for the first flight out to Savannah tonight?"

The man looked about before answering. "Guess it wouldn't do any harm."

The ticket master rustled through his ticket rolls then handed Zeke a ticket. Zeke paid the man plus a little extra.

"Thank you kindly, sir," Zeke said. "Now can you give me directions to that hotel?"

The hotel was a five-minute drive from the terminal, a two-story house renovated to accommodate a few guests and exactly what Zeke needed. He wasn't in the mood for crowds. He parked the steam car then walked up the brick path to the porch. Someone lit a lamp inside as he approached the door.

"Who is it?' a female voice asked.

"Sorry for the late arrival ma'am," Zeke said. "I missed my flight and the ticket master was kind enough to recommend your establishment for an overnight stay."

"Just a minute," the woman said.

Zeke tapped his foot as the woman unlocked the door. He held back a gasp when the woman's face appeared. The dark brown beauty shared a dimpled smile, her hair hidden by a flowered head-wrap. Her housecoat was bound tight around her shapely frame. The ticket master had been modest with his description.

"Well, well, well,' the woman said. "Look who's standing on my doorstep. Zeke Culpepper."

Zeke took off his hat then nodded.

"I'm flattered that my reputation precedes me, especially when it's a woman as pretty as you."

The woman sucked her teeth. "I wonder what Miss Pauline would say about that."

The mention of Pauline brought Zeke out of his moment of distraction.

"I'm looking for a place to stay for the night," he said. "The ticket master said you might have a room to rent."

"That I do," the woman said. "I'm Mary Chestnut."

She extended her hand. Zeke took it then kissed it.

"You already know me," Zeke said.

"Yes, I do. Come on in, Zeke. Would you like some tea?"

Zeke followed Mary into the house.

"If you don't mind," he said. "I know it's late."

Mary turned and smiled. "I don't mind at all. Not for you. Have a seat while I brew us a pot then prepare your room."

The sitting room of Mary's quaint hotel had a homey feel to it. Zeke took a seat on the large sofa as Mary climbed the stairs. He settled into the sofa's inviting cushion, closing his eyes for a brief nap while he waited. Mary returned a few minutes later, waking him.

"Your room is ready," she said. "It's five eagles a night. I take my payment up front."

Zeke whistled. "That's mighty steep for a room."

"It's worth it," Mary replied. "Besides, it's late. Any other hotel would have turned you away."

Zeke took five coins from his money pouch, and then placed them in Mary's hand.

"Why didn't you?" he inquired.

Mary smiled. "Because I have a soft spot for bounty hunters," she said. "Especially you. You saved my life."

Zeke was dumbfounded. "I don't see how I did that. Before tonight, I never laid eyes on you."

Mary sat on the sofa beside him.

"You remember an outlaw who answered to the name of Peter Wainwright?"

A chill passed through Zeke. "Yes, I do. Can't forget that monster. If there ever was a man that needed hanging it was him. My only regret is that I wasn't there to see it."

"I was," Mary said. "I enjoyed every minute of it. I watched him kill my entire family. He would have killed me too if you hadn't showed up and run him off."

Zeke looked puzzled. "Killed your family? Ma'am, I don't . . . wait a minute! You're little Mary Duncan?"

Mary smiled. "That'd be me. I looked younger than I was. I remember you riding up outside our home. That bastard ran to the window then looked outside. A look of terror came to his face then he ran like a rabbit out the back door. You kicked open the door, took me up in your arms then carried me to town."

Zeke looked away. "I wish I'd got there sooner. Took me three more weeks to track him down and bring him in. Lots more people died before I got him."

A shrill whistle interrupted their conversation.

"Tea's ready," Mary said. She sauntered back into the kitchen then returned with a tray. Mary poured tea for both of them then sweetened it with honey. Zeke took a sip then smiled as he closed his eyes.

"This is the best tea I've tasted since my mama passed away,' he said.

"I'm glad you like it," Mary said. "I had the leaves imported from India. You won't find a better tea in Freedonia, probably on this side of the continent."

Zeke drank quickly despite the heat then asked for a refill. As he sipped his eyes met Mary's in a way that made him excited and nervous at the same time.

"So why isn't a fine young lady like you married?" he asked.

"I don't see any reason to be," she said. "I have a good business and a good life. Why would I ruin that with a permanent man?"

"I'm sure you have plenty suitors," he said.

"Zeke Culpepper, are you planning to come courting?"

Zeke finished his tea. "Not me. I'm taken, remember?"

"And if you weren't?" Mary shared a mischievous grin.

Zeke placed down his teacup. "I'm not one that deals with would haves or could haves. Besides, I'm way too old for you."

He yawned unexpectedly, and then covered his mouth.

"Excuse me. Guess I'm sleepier than I thought."

"That's understandable,' Mary said. "You've had a long day. Let me show you to your room."

Zeke followed Mary up the stairs, feeling more sluggish with each step. By the time they reached his room he could barely stand.

"Mary, what the hell is going on?" he said, his voice slurred.

Mary looked at him with a sad expression. "Oh dear, looks like I gave you too much. I'll have to carry you the rest of the way."

Zeke swayed, his vision blurry. "Carry me?"

Mary's face distorted into swirling colors. Zeke took another step toward her, and then collapsed.

* * *

Zeke awoke to sunlight filtering through the sheer curtains of his room. He immediately searched himself; his guns were gone. He sat up then fell back into the bed, his head spinning. Mary had drugged him. His second attempt was more successful. He eased up from the mattress, fighting through the dizzy spell as he stood. A thorough search of the room revealed nothing. Zeke stumbled to the door and attempted to turn the handle.

The door was locked. He sat on the bed then chuckled.

"I'll be damned," he whispered.

"Zeke? Are you awake?"

Mary's voice floated through the door, carrying no hint of her deed.

"Yes, ma'am," he said.

Zeke heard keys rattle, and then the door unlocked.

"Good. Breakfast is ready. Why don't you wash up then come on down? The bathroom is down the hall to the right. Don't tarry. Your food will get cold."

When Zeke opened the door, Mary was gone. He tottered down the hall to the washroom. There was a toothbrush, straight razor and shaving powder waiting. Zeke took his time as he tried to figure out what was going on. It definitely had something to do with Pauline. Mary didn't come off as Spanish, but neither did Pauline. He decided to be calm until he learned more.

Mary waited at the breakfast table, her beauty less pleasant to his eyes due to his circumstances. She wore a simple flowered house dress, her hair bundled over her head and accented with small flowers.

"Good morning, Zeke!" she said. "I hope you slept well."

Zeke sat down before a plate of bacon, eggs and grits. Mary poured him a cup of coffee.

"Didn't have a choice, did I?" he said.

Mary blushed. "I apologize about that. We had to take precautions. You can be a dangerous man."

Zeke took a sip of his coffee, which was excellent. "Who is we?"

Mary didn't answer. Instead she reached down then lifted a leather satchel. She placed it on the table.

"You need to look at what's inside once you finish your breakfast," she said.

Zeke mixed his eggs with his grits. "You work for Miss Tubman, don't you?"

Mary nibbled on her toast. "Sometimes. A woman in my line of work often has access to sensitive information. I was told you were on your way."

"Never trust a ticket master," Zeke said.

Mary smiled. "You were about to cause trouble. We couldn't let that happen."

Zeke crumbled the bacon over the eggs-grits mixture, scooped up a fork full and ate.

"This is mighty good," he said.

"Thank you," Mary replied. "You can't own a hotel unless you're a good cook, or at least have a good cook working for you. The food is a major part of the experience. "

Zeke downed another forkful.

"I figure there are a few of your friends outside to make sure I don't make a break for it."

Mary nodded.

"You figured correct. Now finish your breakfast. We'll talk serious later. Let's enjoy the food and the company."

They ate in silence, Zeke's eyes searching about as he enjoyed his meal. He saw men walking by the windows; the outside was being patrolled. There was nothing else unusual except he was the only guest in the hotel. Miss Mary's establishment had become his prison. For how long he had no idea.

Mary finished her meal first; she waited as Zeke cleared his plate and finished his coffee. Mary stood then picked up the satchel.

"Shall we go into the parlor?"

"As long as you bring this delicious coffee," Zeke said.

Mary extended the satchel to him and he took it.

"I'll get a tray."

Zeke went into the parlor, the satchel tucked under his arm. He opened it as soon as he sat. Inside were papers written in Spanish, quite a few of them paired with Pauline's tintype. There were also quite a few tintypes of Angelo. The image that caught his attention was that of Pauline surrounded by a group of rough looking men and women wearing white linen uniforms and wide brim hats, ammo belts crisscrossing their torsos. Pauline held she held a carbine.

"It seems your sweetheart hasn't been completely honest with you."

Mary ambled into the parlor with the coffee tray. She sat it on the table between them.

"Her real name is Paulina de Rosa," Mary said. "She was known as *La Rosa de Matanzas*, 'The Rose of Matanzas."

"I'll be . . . I mean Lord have mercy."

"She was one the leader of the rebel movement attempting to overthrow the *Nuevo Espana* government in Cuba and declare the island a free nation. Angelo de Silva was her second in command. The main leaders of the revolt were Antonio Maceo and Maximo Gomez."

Zeke's eyebrows rose in surprise. "Angelo wasn't her husband?"

"Not that we know of," Mary replied. "They fled the country when the revolution turned sour. Pauline wanted to remain but the others persuaded her to leave. They hoped she and the others would return to revive the hostilities. Angelo acted as her bodyguard. They gave everyone the married story so not to seem suspicious."

"I've seen them together," Zeke said. "That man was sweet on her."

"His feelings weren't reciprocated as far as we know," Mary said.

Zeke shuffled through the papers trying his best to hide his shock. He had no idea of any of this, but it did explain quite a few things, especially why Pauline was such a good shot.

He pushed the papers away then poured a cup of coffee.

"I'll have to admit I'm surprised by all this," he said. "It still don't change my mind or my intentions."

"Paulina's in New Spain's custody," Mary said. "She's going to be tried then sentenced. There's nothing you can do about it."

"What does Pauline have to do with Freedonia?" Zeke asked. "That's what this is really all about. Why in God's name would Freedonia be concerned with what she did in Cuba?"

"The government feels we need to normalize relations with New Spain," Mary said. "The Spanish suspected she was here for years and petitioned for her extradition. The government ignored them at first, but as relations cooled, they set out to locate her. We've known of her whereabouts for about two years now."

Zeke took another sip of his coffee. "I'm still going after her."

"And do what?" Mary said. "She lied to you, Zeke. If you didn't know this, what else don't you know? She may be a cold-blooded killer!"

"I can't hold that against her, considering what I do for a living."

Mary took his hand. "What you do you do for good, Zeke. You save lives; you saved mine. Let her go. There may be someone better for you in your future."

Zeke leaned back into his chair, studying Mary.

"This ain't about me and Pauline," he said. "This is about me and you."

Mary looked away. "I don't know what you're talking about."

Zeke placed down his cup. "You're sweet on me."

Mary cleared her throat. "I barely know you."

Zeke held his anger in check. For the first time in his life, he wanted to hit a woman.

"If my woman is on her way to prison because of you, then you ain't got a sinner's chance in hell with me. You never did in the first place."

Mary glared at him. "I'm a grown woman, Zeke Culpepper. I never expected you to return my feelings. Hell, you didn't even know I existed until now. Whatever I did it was to protect you. You saved my life. I'm trying to save yours."

Zeke stood then paced the parlor.

"If I try to find her, you're going to kill me?

"I won't, but they will." Mary looked toward the window.

Zeke rubbed his chin as his mind whirled.

"How long y'all plan on keeping me here?"

Mary hand shook as she sipped her coffee. "Until we know you can't cause any trouble."

"So, when y'all are sure Pauline's in Cuba you'll let me go?"

"Yes," Mary said.

"That's not soon enough!"

Zeke lunged at Mary. She tried to hit him, but he blocked her blow then wrapped her up tight in his arms, applying pressure to her neck in just the right place. She passed out in seconds; Zeke lowered her gently onto the parlor couch. He had thirty seconds at the most before she revived so he had to be quick. He ran to his room then hurried into his clothes. He found his guns in Mary's room at the foot of her bed. The bullets and shells were on her dresser. He loaded the guns as he made his way for the front door. He waited until the guard was almost to the door then jerked it open. The guard's eyes went wide just before Zeke hit him on the forehead with the butt of his shotgun. He holstered the shotgun then grabbed the man's rifle. He took careful aim at the guard patrolling the perimeter then fired, grazing the man's head. He fell onto the porch unconscious. Zeke crouched as he heard the other guards running toward him, their boots pounding hard on the wraparound porch. The guard to his left appeared first; Zeke shot him in the leg then twisted in time to shoot the second guard in the leg as well. After disarming both men he ran to the back for his steam car. He sped around the house into gunfire. Mary knelt on the porch, firing with intent to kill. Zeke made it out shaken but unscathed. As the hotel faded into the distance behind him, his thoughts shifted to saving Pauline. He had to catch up with her, and he knew exactly where to go to do it.

- 4 -

The *Palmetto Express* hissed to a stop at the main terminal in Savannah, Gullahland. Pauline opened her eyes to Philippe snoring before her. She twisted to look out the cabin window. The station was fairly empty at such an early hour, the platform wet from a recent rain. A group of women dressed in white cotton dresses and colorful headwraps set up tables, carrying baskets of fresh fruits and vegetables balanced on their heads. Gullahland's roots were closer to the Caribbean and West Africa, which reflected in the local lifestyle and their lilting patois. In the early days of Freedonia most thought this region would strike out as its own nation or at least petition for self-autonomy like the Cherokee controlled Echota. However, the Gullahland Elders met under their massive meeting tree in St. Helena and voted to be a part of the new nation to the relief of Freedonia's leaders. Savannah, Charleston and Wilmington were all part of the region, valuable harbors which supported Freedonia's sea trade with the rest of the world.

She had to get away. A death sentence waited for her in Cuba. Once she was free, she would leave Freedonia. She was foolish to think she would be safe forever, despite having evaded detection for ten years. A plan formed in her head; she would head north through America then into Canada. Once there, she would go west, her destination Oregon. It was a wild and dangerous territory, the perfect place for a woman with a price on her head to hide.

Philippe stirred, and then opened his eyes. A sleazy smile came to his face as his bleary orbs focused on her.

"*Buenos dias*, Paulina," he said, his voice gravelly. "I must say you are a beautiful sight to wake up to."

"I can't say the same," she replied.

Philippe performed an exaggerated stretch, and then yawned.

"What can I say? God did not bless me with a handsome face. But He was generous with other talents, which is why you sit before me in your splendor."

"I need to freshen up," she said.

"Of course," Philippe replied.

Pauline raised her handcuffed wrists. "I can't it with these."

"I'm no fool," Philippe said. "You'll have to manage."

He opened the cabin door.

"José!"

José stuck his bald head into the cabin.

"Si, Philippe?"

"Please escort Miss De Rosa to the lavatory and keep a close eye on her."

José nodded. Pauline walked to the lavatory, José close behind. As soon as she closed the door, she tried the window. It was bolted shut. She gazed through the dingy glass to access her situation. The platform filled with travelers, most dressed in the traditional white cotton garments of the Gullah. She gave up on the window escape, and then washed up as well as she could. She brushed by José as she walked back to her cabin. She hesitated before Philippe's cabin as if to enter then bolted toward the train exit.

"Help me! Help me!" she screamed as she ran. Pauline reached the exit, scrambled down the narrow stairs then jumped onto the platform. She raised her shackled wrists as she ran toward a group of merchant women she spied through the bathroom window. The Gullah folk gathered around her, their faces filled with sympathy and disgust.

Philippe and his men exited the train onto the platform.

"Get away from her!" Philippe shouted. "This woman is in the custody of New Spain."

"Slavers!" one of the women shouted. The crowd surged toward Philippe and his henchmen. They scrambled back onto the train. The Gullah folk shouted and shook their fists, some of them throwing vegetables and whatever they could find at the train.

One of the women, a tall rotund beauty, hugged Pauline like a child.

"Don't you worry, sister," she said in her lilting patois. "We'll get you safe."

The women formed a protective barrier around her as they hurried her out of the station. A group of young men were gathered under the broad canopy of a nearby live oak, talking and teasing each other.

"Jeremiah!" the woman shouted.

One of the boys lifted his head then tilted back his straw hat.

"Yes, ma'am?"

"Go fetch the wagon!" the woman shouted.

The boy sprinted away.

"What's your name, sugar?" the woman asked.

"Pauline," she said.

"I'm Barbara," the woman said. "This here is Martha, Bessie, Daisy and Christine. Don't you worry none. We're going to take you where you'll be safe."

Jeremiah pulled up moments later in the wagon.

"Bessie, you and Jeremiah take Miss Pauline to Tybee," Barbara said. "Mama Mary will fix everything."

"Yes, ma'am," Bessie and Jeremiah said in unison.

Constables arrived on horseback and in wagons, heading for the ruckus on the platform.

"Go now!" Barbara said.

"Git on, mule!" Jeremiah said as he snapped the reins. The mule snorted a brief protest then sauntered away from the commotion, easing Pauline to safety. She looked back to the station as more constables arrived to control the growing mob. She closed her eyes then said a prayer for forgiveness. The accusation of slavery was one of the worst charges anyone could level on another in Freedonia, especially in Gullahland.

"You going to be alright, ma'am," Jeremiah said. "I'll protect you."

The boy's bravado made Pauline smile. She wouldn't be safe until she was out of Freedonia.

"Thank you so much," she said.

"Where you from?" Bessie asked.

Bessie blinked her large brown eyes, an innocent smile on her pretty umber face. Pauline could barely remember being so young. She did remember that she was never that innocent.

"Hapeville," Pauline answered.

"Where's that?"

"Leave Miss Pauline alone, girl," Jeremiah said. "You always asking questions."

"How else I'm supposed to learn anything, boy?" she said.

"You'll have to excuse Bessie," Jeremiah said to Pauline. "She's always sticking her nose in somebody else's business."

"And you always trying to tell somebody what to do," Bessie snapped.

"That's okay," Pauline said. "I don't mind the questions. Bessie's entitled to ask me anything she wants."

"Yes I am!" Bessie said. She hit Jeremiah's head.

"To answer your question Bessie, Hapeville is a small town about ten miles south of Atlanta."

Pauline didn't think Bessie's eyes could get wider, but they did.

"Atlanta! You've been to Atlanta? You have got to tell me about Atlanta!"

"You done set her off now, Miss Pauline," Jeremiah said. "I ain't never seen a person love a place so much where she ain't never been."

"You don't have to go to a place to love it," Bessie retorted. "I read about it all the time in the *GullahGazette*. They say almost two hundred thousand people live there. And I heard the Peachtree Theater hosts the best shows in all Freedonia!"

"There are a lot of people living in Atlanta," Pauline said. "But I can't vouch for the shows. I'm not much of a theater person."

"How can you not like the theater?" Bessie said. "All that wonderful dancing and singing?"

"I don't like the theater either," Jeremiah said.

"That's different," Bessie said to him. "You're country and stupid. Miss Pauline is a sophisticated lady like me."

They fell silent as another group of constables rode by.

"Them must be some bad Spaniards," Bessie said. "I ain't never seen that many constables come calling. Most of the time you can't get them to drop an apple to do their job."

Jeremiah laughed loud. "You ain't never lied!"

Pauline laughed as well, the first time since she'd been captured.

"Miss Bertha told me to take you to Mama Mary, but we have to make a stop first," Jeremiah said.

Bessie turned to glare at Jeremiah. "You better not be going for no cigars."

"Shows how much you know." Jeremiah smiled at Pauline. "I'm taking you by Mr. Jones's shop. Got to get those shackles off."

Pauline looked at her wrists. She'd worn the handcuffs so long she'd forgotten them. Was it that easy to get used to bondage? She thought of her friends in Cuba and the solemn mood took over again.

"Thank you, Jeremiah. I wish we could remove all the shackles everywhere."

If the young ones heard her last words they didn't respond. They kept to the main road for another half an hour before veering onto a grassy path cut by wagon wheel ruts. The path led to a wooden home shadowed by a large live oak bearded with Spanish moss. Metal littered the ground surrounding it; wheels, panels, gates, and fence parts lay in various states of repair. A few had rusted in place. The door swung open and a man ducked under the frame as he emerged. Mr. Jones was the classic blacksmith; black skinned, tall and broad shouldered. Flecks of grayshimmered in his black hair, a ragged beard rimming his broad chin. He reached into the front pocket of his leather apron then extracted a dingy cloth, wiping his hands.

"What you doing here, Lil' Bit?" he said. "And who that with you?"

"How you doing sir," Jeremiah said. "This here is Miss Pauline."

Jeremiah pulled the wagon to a stop. He jumped out the wagon then helped Pauline out.

"You ain't never helped me out the wagon," Bessie commented.

"Hush up now!" Jeremiah replied.

"See? Always trying to tell somebody what to do!"

"Y'all children quit fussing," Mr. Jones said. He extended his hand. "How you doing, Miss Pauline?"

Pauline extended her shackled hands. "Not too well, Mr. Jones."

Mr. Jones's welcoming face twisted into an expression of anger.

"I'll be damned," he said. "Y'all come on back."

Pauline, Jeremiah and Bessie followed Mr. Jones into his house. It was a cluttered mess, filled with more iron strewn about.

"My name is Peter Jones," he said. "Folks around here call me Big Pete."

"I'm very pleased to meet you, Big Pete," Pauline said.

Big Pete chuckled. “Most folks in your situation usually are.”

“Is this going to hurt?”

Big Pete walked over to a cluttered cabinet then pulled open one of the drawers.

“Not this time,” he said. “I always keep these handy.”

Big Pete held up a ring of lock pickers. Jeremiah pulled out a chair for Pauline and Bessie. Big Pete slid his chair in front of Pauline then took her hands.

“These don’t look like slave hands,” he commented. “Working hands, but not slave hands.”

Pauline’s throat tightened. “How would you know?”

Pete chuckled again. “Now don’t you worry none, Miss Pauline. “I ain’t one to judge or ask questions. There’s a good reason I live way back in these woods.”

“Sure is!” Jeremiah said. “Mr. Jones use to be a . . .”

“Hush up now, Lil’ Bit,” Big Pete said. “Ain’t your place to talk about business that ain’t yours.”

Jeremiah lowered his head, his shoulders slumping. “Yes sir.”

Bessie leaned away from him, her eyes narrow. “And you say I talk too much.”

Pauline watched Big Pete working his way through the different lock picks.

“So how do you know slave hands?” she asked.

“You know there ain’t no more slaves in Freedonia,” Big Pete answered. “Echota, either.”

“I know,” Pauline replied.

“But they’re still some up North, in America,” he said.

"I thought America banned the slave trade."

"It's all about the words," Pete said. "They banned the slave trade, but they didn't ban slavery. All them slave holders we ran out of Freedonia settled in up in West America. They can't bring in any more Africans, but they don't have to let go those they took with them. So, every now and then I get a man, woman or child showing up just like you."

"America's not the only place with slaves," Pauline said, anger clear on her face.

"If President Douglass gets his way, there won't be one enslaved African this side of the Atlantic."

"I hope he gets his way," Pauline said.

Big Pete stopped shuffling through the picks.

"Yeah, this one will do."

Pete worked at the lock until the handcuffs clicked open. It was the best sound Pauline had heard in a long time. She wrapped her arms around Big Pete's neck then kissed him on the cheek.

"Thank you so much, Big Pete," she said.

Big Pete laughed. "First time I've been kissed for picking a lock."

The trio hurried back to the wagon, Big Pete strolling behind them.

"Y'all tell Mama Mary I said hey," he said.

"We will," Bessie and Jeremiah chimed.

"Thank you again," Pauline said.

Big Pete nodded. "You stay out of trouble, little lady."

Pauline smiled. "I'll try."

They returned to the main road and continued their journey to Mama Mary's, reaching the small white home on the edge of the marsh at dusk. An ancient live oak shadowed the modest building like most of the homes in the region. The house was painted white with blue trim around the window and a blue door. Mama Mary sat on her front porch, rocking back and forth in her rocking chair as she smoked a pipe. A halo of gray hair graced her head, matching the white blouse and skirt. Jeremiah guided the wagon to the hitching post then secured the mule as Bessie and Pauline climbed down.

"Hey Mama Mary," Bessie said.

"Hey baby," Mama Mary replied. "Who this you got with you?"

Mama Mary's melodious voice reminded Pauline of Jamaica. The woman shared a comforting smile with Pauline but her eyes were more discriminating.

Mama Mary stood as Pauline climbed the brick stairs. She hugged the small woman like a long lost relative.

"*Buenas noches*," Mama Mary whispered.

Pauline jumped in surprise to Mama Mary's response. How did she know?

Jeremiah ran up then jumped onto the porch.

"She's a runaway," he said. "Miss Bertha told us to bring her out here so she could lay low."

"Y'all done good," Mama Mary said. "Go out back and get you some water. I got some turnip greens and carrots for your folks, too. Take what you need."

"Thank you, Mama Mary!" Bessie said. The two hurried to the back of the house.

"Now you grab a seat and tell me what you really running from," Mama Mary said.

Pauline found another rocking chair then pulled it beside Mama Mary. She sat then rocked in time with the matriarch.

"I'm not a slave," Pauline said.

"I suspected as much," Mary replied. "Ain't been no slavery around here in a long time, and your clothes are too new for you to be from up North. My grandparents were slaves. They fought in the Liberation. Folks around here still real sensitive about it, though. Them sugar plantations were hell. It was a good reason for getting away from somebody, especially somebody white."

"How did you know I was from New Spain?" Pauline asked.

"You got that look," Mary said.

Pauline didn't try to figure that out. She'd met women like Mama Mary before. They possessed a talent that couldn't be explained. She could be a powerful friend or enemy.

"I got in some serious trouble in Cuba a long time ago," Pauline said. "I ran away from it but my past caught up with me a few days ago."

"The past has a way of doing that," Mama Mary said. "Sometimes it happens for a reason."

Mama Mary's gaze made Pauline uncomfortable. She looked away as she rocked.

"I won't bother you long," Pauline said. "I need to get away. If you could just let me rest here for the night, I'd be grateful."

"Of course you can," Mama Mary said. "I ain't never denied nobody a safe haven. What you plan on doing afterwards?"

"I don't know. I'll probably head north to Canada, probably Montreal," Pauline said. "I'll find some kind of work, at least long enough to save up enough money to head west. I'm thinking Oregon would be a good place to stay."

"That's wild country out there," Mama Mary said. "Dangerous, too."

"A perfect place to hide," Pauline replied.

Bessie and Jeremiah returned with bright faces and armfuls of produce.

"We really appreciate you, Mama Mary!" Bessie said.

Mary placed her pipe down on a low table beside her chair.

"Y'all think y'all can give Mama a kiss without dropping anything?"

Bessie and Jeremiah shuffled over to Mama Mary and kissed her cheeks.

"Bye Mama! Bye Miss Pauline!" Bessie said as climbed down the stairs.

"You'll be alright now," Jeremiah said. "As safe as a gator in a mud hole."

Pauline stood then kissed Jeremiah on his cheek. Jeremiah almost dropped his vegetables.

"Thank you for protecting me," she said.

Jeremiah glided off the porch, looking back at Pauline with a dreamy smile.

Mama Mary chuckled.

"Now why you go do that? He's going to be a mess for at least a week."

Mama Mary grunted as she stood.

"You best come on in now. I'll get you something to sleep in and show you your room. I hope you don't mind sleeping in an old lady's nightgown. When I was your age, I didn't sleep in them much at all. Especially if there was a man close by."

Mary and Pauline exchanged a smile.

"I suspect you were a handful back then," Pauline said.

"According to some two hands full," Mary replied.

The women shared a mischievous laugh.

"Come on and follow me," Mary said. She led Pauline to the washroom at the rear of the house.

"I'll see you in the morning," Mary said. "These old bones need their rest."

"Thank you so much," Pauline replied.

Mary waved her hand. "Ain't nothing. You get some rest now."

Pauline worked the water pump handle, filling the sink with cool water. She took her time washing up, relaxing with the ritual. She used the rose water sitting on the counter to freshen up then put on the gown. It was too big, but would suffice for one night. Miss Mary's guestroom was a tiny thing, just wide enough to hold the bed and dresser inside. It was as if the room was built around the bed. Pauline shuffled inside then fell into the soft mattress. As she snuggled in the tension fell away. She was safe for at least one night.

In the morning, she would be on her way. An image of Zeke's face appeared in her mind and she held back a sigh. She would miss him, but she had to go. There was no choice.

- 5 -

Zeke maneuvered his steam car up the path leading to June Bug's house, weaving around water filled potholes and scattered granite stones. He was exhausted from the long journey; Macon was a good one hundred miles from Hapeville, four days of driving with few rest stops in between. As he neared the immaculate brick home hidden behind a wall of oak trees, he realized he could be wasting his time. June Bug might not be home; he was a traveling man who enjoyed the road more than staying in one place. He was also in high demand because he was the smartest man this side of Tuskegee Institute, some said second only to George Washington Carver. June Bug was also a criminal, another man who owed his current standing to Zeke. It was time to call in a favor.

Zeke approached the front of the house then honked his horn. It turned out to be his lucky day. The front door opened and June Bug stepped onto the porch, followed by his wife and two of his children. He was an imposing man with chestnut brown skin, at least six feet five inches tall and built like he was made to throw boulders at the sky. His wife, Ceely, was almost as tall, a dark brown beauty and as feminine as June Bug was masculine. God rarely created folks like June Bug and Ceely, but when He did, He did it well.

Zeke smiled as June Bug shielded his eyes from the noonday sun.

"Ezekiel Culpepper! Is that you driving up my path?"

His booming voice cut through the chatter of the steam engine. Zeke waited until he pulled up to the porch and shut off the engine before answering.

"Nobodybut." Zeke climbed out the car, and-then folded his arms across his chest. "Damn June Bug! You're as ugly as the last time I saw you."

He took off his hat then bowed to Ceely.

"How you doing, Miss Ceely?"

Ceely smiled. "I'm good, Zeke. What brings you down this way?"

Zeke leaned against his car. "I woke up a week ago and decided I needed to see beauty. So I came to see you."

Ceely laughed and June Bug frowned.

"You know I don't like you flirting with my wife," June Bug said.

"Ain't no harm in it," Ceely replied. "You know I ain't got no interest in Zeke. Now if he was two feet taller . . ."

They all laughed. Zeke was happy for the humorous respite, but the reason for his visit resurfaced with immediacy.

"I need your help, June Bug," Zeke said. "I need to get to Savannah and I need to get there fast."

"You need the dragonfly?" June Bug asked.

"Sure do."

"Ceely, take the kids out back," June Bug said.

Ceely gathered the children then herded them to the backyard. June Bug lumbered down the porch stairs then walked up to Zeke. He folded his arms across his massive chest.

"Zeke, you know the life I used to lead. I'm mighty thankful for you giving me a chance to turn it around. I know you did it because you're a God-fearing man. I owe you for that."

Zeke looked up into June Bug's face. "Yes you do. Let's get going."

"That's just it," June Bug said. "It's against the law for a man like me to own a dragonfly."

"Since when did a man like you listen to the law?" Zeke asked.

"Since two years ago," June Bug replied.

Zeke pushed back his hat. "What are you saying, June Bug?"

"I sold it."

Zeke pushed back his hat further. "To who?"

"That's not important," June Bug said. "The main thing is that it's gone."

"I need that dragonfly," Zeke said. "It's a matter of life or death."

June Bug rubbed his chin.

"Whose?"

"A young woman named Pauline Rose."

"So you're helping somebody out like you helped me?"

"That's it," Zeke said.

"Well that's different," June Bug said. "Follow me."

Zeke followed the big man around the back. Ceely and the children played tag as the men walked by. Ceely stopped, her large brown eyes narrowed.

"Horace? What's going on?"

"It's okay, Ceely," June Bug replied.

"Horace?" Zeke said. "Your name is Horace?"

"Ceely calls me Horace," he said. "You call me June Bug."

They walked to the barn. June Bug unlatched the doors then swung them open. Zeke could see the Dragonfly before entering.

"You told me you sold it! You big liar!"

June Bug shrugged.

"It's ready to fly," he said. "I've made some improvements in the aerodynamics and increased engine efficiency. This baby will go twice as fast as a government dragonfly and get three times the distance on a gallon of fuel. All it needs is kerosene, and that's the problem."

"Why is that a problem?" Zeke said.

"You know how much kerosene it takes to fly this thing? Anybody buying that much fuel is going to raise suspicions."

"So, we won't buy it," Zeke said.

June Bug frowned. "I'm an honest man now, Zeke."

"Yeah, an honest man who just lied to my face. You'll be fine," Zeke said. "You just get ready to fly me to Savannah. I'll get the kerosene."

"I can't let you do that, Zeke," June Bug said. "That would be wrong."

"You ain't letting me do anything," Zeke replied. "I'm doing what I need to do, and if you try to stop me, I'll shoot you in the foot."

June Bug raised his hands in surrender.

"I tried, Lord," he said.

Zeke strolled back to his car.

"I'll be back in two days or I won't be back at all," Zeke said.

"You be careful now, Zeke," June Bug said. "And don't break too many laws."

"Whatever it takes," Zeke said. "I love that woman, and I'm going to get her back."

Kerosene. The only thing that stood between him and seeing Pauline again. He started the steam car.

"Just how do you plan on getting that kerosene, Zeke?" June Bug asked.

"They still got that casino in Forsyth?"

"I wouldn't know," June Bug said.

Zeke put his hands on his waist then squinted at June Bug.

June Bug laughed. "They shut it down three years ago. Sheriff Bodeen wasn't getting his cut so he busted it up."

"I need to find a card game, June Bug. That kind of atmosphere draws the type of people I need to see."

"You're playing with fire, Zeke," June Bug warned.

Zeke grinned. "Don't I always?"

"And since when did you become good at poker?" June Bug asked.

"I ain't going to win," Zeke said. "I'm going to find out where I can get kerosene."

June Bug looked left then right before speaking.

"There's a new gambling house about five miles outside of Macon on Lake Tobasofkee," he said. "They're doing it right and making Bodeen happy. He don't pay it no mind as long as they keep the death toll to a minimum and nobody important gets hurt."

"Then that's where I'm headed," Zeke said.

"Don't take your automobile," June Bug advised. "Those boys would kill you and roll you in the lake for that thing before you got there good. You can take one of my horses."

"The car is faster," Zeke said.

"You can't save your lady friend if you're dead."

"I don't have time for this," Zeke said. "I have to go."

"Nobody's going anywhere, at least not today."

Ceely entered the barn then placed her hands on her shapely hips.

"Zeke Culpepper, I know you just didn't come all this way to insult my man, tell me how pretty I am and then leave!"

"Yes I did, Ceely," Zeke answered. "I plan on coming back though. Me and June Bug got business to tend to."

"You'll be staying the night," Ceely announced. "I've already cut up an extra chicken and we have a guest room for visitors, which we don't get to use often. So you just cool your heels and get ready to stay a spell."

"Ceely, I don't mean to be rude but . . ."

"Then don't," Ceely said.

Zeke looked to June Bug for help but his friend shrugged his shoulders.

"You ain't gonna win, so you might as well get your things and stay the night. "

"This is life or death," Zeke said. "I have to go. Now."

Ceely's eyes widened. "You're serious, Zeke?"

"Yes, I am, Ceely," Zeke said. "The sooner I get going the better."

"You go on then," Ceely said. "And be careful around them gamblers."

Zeke climbed into his car, speeding off in a cloud of steam and dust. Every moment without seeing Pauline was another step closer to not seeing her ever again. Time was getting shorter and shorter. He had to make the most of it.

- 6 -

Pauline awoke with the rooster's crow. She stretched, yawned then rubbed her eyes as she smiled. It was almost like waking at home. She had a notion to feed the chickens and milk the cows but the reality of her situation returned. She sighed, eased out of the big bed then dressed, anxious to be on her way. The sooner she left the better.

She heard footsteps outside the room as she buttoned her blouse. Apparently Mama Mary was up as well. Pauline opened the door then stopped in her tracks. Mama Mary stood in the middle of her kitchen, a shotgun in her hands. She put a finger to her lips then waved Pauline to her side.

"I think we got visitors," she whispered. "Old Billy don't ever crow this early. Laziest rooster in Gullahland. Reach into my pocket."

Pauline did as she was told. Her hand touched a pistol grip; she extracted a Colt revolver. She reached into Mary's pocket again with her left hand and took out a handful of bullets.

"I'm guessing you know how to use it?" Mary said.

Pauline nodded as she loaded the Colt.

"We'll wait here to see if they'll come knocking. If they do, we'll be ready for them."

"No," Pauline said. "They're here for me and I won't let you risk your life because of trouble I brought."

"What you going to do?" Mary asked.

"The best defense is a good offense," Pauline said.

She kissed Mama Mary's cheek. "Thank you for everything. I won't forget you."

"God bless you, Pauline," Mama Mary said.

Pauline crept to the front door. She eased the door open then crawled onto the porch. She stopped, scanning the area. There were too many places an interloper could hide and she was unfamiliar with the farm. She would have to draw them out. If it was Gonzales and his boys, they intended to capture her, not kill her. Her intentions were just the opposite.

She stood then stomped hard down the stairs before running toward the marsh.

"Ahi estaella!"

Three men sprang from the shadows. Pauline slowed then peeked over her shoulder; they were bunched together as she hoped. She spun about, dropped to her knees, and then began shooting. Two of the men went down; Pauline cursed as the old gun jammed before she could get off a third shot. She threw the gun aside as the third man rushed her.

Pauline kicked the man in the gut then landed an uppercut to his chin as he doubled over. The man staggered back then quickly recovered. He was a skilled fighter, coming at her with jabs and kicks. Pauline deftly avoided his attack, dodging and sidestepping his blows, striking him with jabs and punches of her own. The man threw a hard hook at her head; Pauline ducked the blow as she whirled then swept the man off his feet. She was about to kick him in the temple when a loud blast shattered the morning quiet.

Pauline turned to see Mama Mary on the front porch. Gonzales stood beside her, her shotgun in his hands. Pauline couldn't see his face clearly but she knew he grinned.

"Enough of this," he said. "You will come with us or I will kill your friend."

Pauline's shoulders slumped. She raised her hands over her head; the man she was about to kill struck her jaw hard and she fell forward.

"Jorge!" Gonzales shouted. "Hit her one more time and I'll kill you!"

"She killed our men!" Jorge shouted.

'"Don't touch her again!" Gonzales replied. "Tie her hands and let's go. We'll miss out boat!"

Jorge yanked her arms behind her back, and then tied her tight. He shoved her toward Gonzales and Mama Mary.

"I'm so sorry," Mary said.

"It's not your fault," Pauline replied. "Thank you for your help."

Gonzales let Mary go. He led Pauline to a waiting horse then helped her into the saddle.

"This was inevitable," Gonzales said. "No more running. No more hiding. You and the others will pay for your crimes."

Pauline spat on Gonzales's right boot. The general laughed.

"Come now," he said. "There's no reason to be uncivil," he said. "We have a long journey ahead of us."

"And yours will end at the end of a rope!" Jorge said.

"Be quiet, Jorge!" George said. "We will conduct ourselves in a pleasant manner despite Señorita Rosa's behavior. There will be plenty of time for unpleasantness later."

He turned to Mama Mary then shot her. Pauline screamed as the old woman tumbled into her house.

"You bastard!" Pauline shouted.

Gonzales smiled.

"This is your fault. If you had not tried to escape the woman would still be alive."

Rage kept Pauline silent. The cruelty of New Spain coursed through Gonzales's veins. It was the reason she joined the revolution. It would be the reason she joined again.

It was a long, silent ride back to Savannah. The noonday sun drove away the morning chill, making for a mild winter day. Curious eyes followed the trio through the city to the docks. Pauline saw the waiting passenger ship and her mood darkened. There was no escape now. She was on her way back to Cuba to face her past.

A steamship flying the flag of New Spain rocked with the gentle tides. A group of Freedonian soldiers and a middle-aged umber gentleman in a gray suit and top hat stood at the docks. The man's dignified appearance caught Pauline's attention; he was probably a diplomat or wealthy merchant. The gentleman and the soldiers watched Pauline, Gonzales and Jorge. Hope emerged as they dismounted and the gentleman approached followed by the soldiers. It was quickly dashed when the suited man reached out and shook Gonzales's hand.

"Ambassador Green, it is good see you," Gonzales said.

"Good to see you too, Colonel. I'm heading back to Cuba so I decided to join you."

The ambassador looked over Gonzales's shoulder to Pauline.

"I see your business here is complete."

"Yes, it is," Gonzales answered. "It's still a mystery to me that your government waited so long to share Señorita de Rosa's whereabouts."

The ambassador waved his hand as if driving away a fly. "That doesn't matter now. Freedonia promised its full cooperation and we delivered. I would say this sordid episode is over."

"Yes, it is, Ambassador."

"If you'll excuse me, I must get to my cabin," Green said. "See you in Havana?"

"Of course," Gonzales replied. "Good day, ambassador."

Ambassador Green and his escort proceeded up the walkway onto the ship. Pauline followed him with angry eyes. She was about to hurl an expletive at him until something strange happened. The ambassador looked at her, and then winked. Her first instinct was that the gesture was an added insult, but there was something about his face that signaled a deeper meaning.

"Let's go," Gonzales said. "We tried to be nice, but you just won't cooperate. Your accommodations will be a bit less pleasant than on the train."

They boarded the ship. Gonzales grinned as he leaned toward her. Pauline jerked her head away, the kiss meant for her lips glancing her cheek.

Gonzales seemed unfazed. "This is where we part company. The next time I see you we'll be in Cuba. Jorge, take her to her room."

"With pleasure," Jorge said.

Jorge shoved her into the ship then down to the lowest deck. They continued through the narrow hallway to a small cabin near the engine room.

"Welcome home," he said. He opened the door, shoved her into the room and then slammed the door. Pauline heard Jorge lock the door. She rubbed her raw wrists, thankful that he had at least untied her.

The room contained a cot and a chair. She shuddered as she sat on the cot. Despair attempted to overwhelm her but she fought it back. It was not over yet. As long as she was alive, she had a chance. And Ambassador Green's wink meant something. She had a feeling she wouldn't know until they reached Cuba.

If Pauline thought Gonzales would be easy during their journey, she was wrong. The Cuban officer wouldn't allow her out of the room. Her food was brought to her by Jorge, who watched her eat every bite with her hands. Apparently, Gonzales did not trust her with utensils. He took the plate when she was done. A bucket was supplied to her for waste which was taken away by an obviously unhappy steward. It was a prison within the luxury liner, a situation she was not unfamiliar with. She kept track of the days by the coming and going of the sliver of sunlight which sneaked into her room through an unpainted window patch. Pauline distracted herself with thoughts of her farm and Zeke. It was a lovely, sedate life and Zeke was the final piece making it perfect. He wasn't a perfect man, but who was she to complain? He was trying his best to make a better life which was all she could ask. Gloom invaded her mind like a black storm cloud. It didn't matter now; she was on her way back to answer to the sins of a past life. A part of her knew this day would come. Her enemies were relentless and she'd caused so much death and damage.

Pauline noticed a shift in the momentum of the steamship. She stood, concentrating on the motion. She couldn't be sure, but it seemed the ship was slowing. She knew how long it took to sail to Cuba; they should be reaching Havana harbor by sunset. This was an early stop.

The sound of shouting, screaming and shooting reached her makeshift cell. The urgent voices increased; soon the voices were outside the door. Pauline hunted her room for something to use as a weapon, realizing that if whoever came through the door was armed with a gun her effort would be in vain. Still, she refused to go down without a fight. She settled on the water pitcher, dumping its contents into her waste bucket then raising it over her head, poised to strike.

The door flew open, smashing against the wall. A man staggered in backward, and then turned to face her. It was Jorge. He snarled at her, and then his face went slack. He fell to the floor, a machete protruding from his back. A man with a blue scarf wrapped around his face leapt over Jorge's body, another machete in his right hand, a revolver in his left.

"It's her!" he shouted. "It's Paulina!"

The man tucked the revolver in his waist belt the removed his scarf. A wide grin broke across his grizzled face.

"Pauline! Do you not recognize me?"

Pauline squinted as she shuffled through a cache of memories. She jerked as the man's face appeared in her mind, a younger clean-shaven version of the one standing before her.

"Diego?" she said. "Is that you?"

Pauline dropped the water pitcher as Diego rushed to her, lifting her in the air and spinning around.

"Yes, yes!" he shouted.

He placed her back on her feet.

"Come, we must go," he said. "We don't have much time."

Diego handed Pauline the machete then took the revolver from his belt. Pauline followed her rescuer and old friend. Twelve armed men stood on deck, holding rifles and revolvers on the crew and passengers. A cheer rose from the men as she emerged; Pauline smiled and nodded at them. Gonzales was among the passengers. He glared at her, hands on his head, his face red. She searched among the others then spotted the Freedonian ambassador. His hands were raised like the others and he smiled. He nodded when their eyes met.

"Come," Diego said, pulling at her arm. "We must go."

Pauline followed Diego to the bulwark. A rope ladder dangled from the rail to a pair of motorized fishing boats idling on the calm waves. Pauline climbed down into one of the boats. The steersman removed his scarf, revealing another face she recognized immediately.

"Ramirez!"

Ramirez nodded and smiled.

"Ramirez, what's happening? How did you know I'd be on this ship?" she asked.

"It is a long story," he said. "We will tell you everything once you are safe."

She sat still as the others clambered down the ladder and into the boats. No sooner was the last man settled did the boats turn abruptly then speed across the water toward the island that had been Pauline's home and battlefield for so long. All the men took off their scarves; some faces Pauline recognized, some she didn't. One thing she did know was that she was among friends. What she didn't understand was why.

"My comrades!" Diego shouted. "Victory is at hand. La Rosa de Matanzas has returned!"

- 7 -

Clementine's lurked in a cove near the banks of Lake Tobasofskee; a two-story white building resembling the grand plantation houses that existed before the Liberation. The porch gas lights cast their glow on the lake like ghostly fishermen, the illumination occasionally dispersed by a breeze skimming the surface of the clear waters. Lively music accented by raunchy lyrics drifted up through the pines, white oak and dogwood trees hiding the establishment from casual eyes.

Zeke drove as far down the road leading to Clementine's as he could before it became too narrow. He didn't know how he was going to leave the casino; if he had to run, he didn't want to run too far. Zeke knew his gambling skills were less than stellar. There was no way he could earn the amount of money needed to buy enough kerosene to get him to Savannah. He had only one option: he had to rob Clementine's.

He worked the cross hanging from his neck between his fingers as he climbed out of the car then checked his revolvers and shotgun. Satisfied, he pinched the cross between his fingers then closed his eyes.

"Lord, I didn't come here to kill nobody," he prayed. "And you know I ain't the kind of man that would break a law on purpose. But I'm very fond of Pauline and I need to find her and bring her back home. I hope you understand if things get out of hand. Amen"

He tucked the cross into his shirt, shoved his revolvers into his shoulder holsters, and then slid his shotgun to its leg holster. Putting on his jacket, he climbed out of his car and sauntered down the road, avoiding the water puddles caused by a recent rain. By the time he reached Clementine he was resolved.

He did a quick scan of the building; apparently Clementine's hosted a genteel clientele for there were no guards outside. The situation was different as he reached the entrance. Two burly men dressed in tuxedos met Zeke at the door, each man cradling Henri rifles in their arms with Colts resting on their hips. They were Creek warriors; Zeke recognized the small tattoos on their cheeks. Their eyes went to his shotgun.

"Welcome to Clementine's," one of the guards said. "We're going to have to ask you to leave your weapon with us."

Zeke was hoping to do this without bloodshed, but it looked like that wasn't going to be possible.

"I'm not sure I can do that," Zeke answered.

The guards began to shift their rifles but Zeke was faster. His shotgun was in his hand and pointed at them.

"I don't want no trouble," he said.

"Then why start it, Ezekiel Culpepper?"

The voice came from his left. Zeke spun to see three more guards with their Henri rifles trained on him. The gentleman who spoke stood among them dressed in a fine suit and derby, a ponytail draped over his right shoulder. He smiled as he tipped his hat. Zeke cursed silently; he was slipping. There was no way that many people would have snuck up on him if he was in his right mind. Worrying about Pauline and her whereabouts was affecting his skills.

"This is disappointing," the gentleman said. "I hoped to meet the famous Zeke Culpepper one day but under much better circumstances."

Zeke lowered his shotgun. There was no way he could shoot his way out of this situation; a little persuasion and a lot of prayer were in order.

"You know my name," he said. "But I haven't had the privilege to learn yours."

"Hassa Ola," the man said. "I'm the owner of this establishment."

"A mighty fine place you got here."

"Yes, it is," Hassa Ola replied. "It keeps our people well-financed. By the looks of it you didn't come to gamble. I think you came to rob us, which disappoints me. I expected better of you. I heard you're a church going man."

"That I am," Zeke said. "As I hope you are. I think a little forgiveness would be appreciated right now."

Hassa and his men laughed.

"Forgiveness in these parts is usually a bullet to the forehead and a slow trip to the bottom of the lake," Hassa said. "But I have a proposition for you, Zeke Culpepper, something that would be mutually beneficial for both of us."

Zeke perked up. He might just get out of this situation alive.

"I'm listening."

"There's a man in Macon that owes me a lot of money. I'm willing to pay you to find him and bring him to me."

"How much?" Zeke asked.

Hassa Ola grinned. "Your life."

"Sounds reasonable," Zeke said. "How can you be sure I'll honor my debt?"

"Like I said, I hear you're an honest man. I also know you need a fair amount of kerosene that I'm willing to provide."

"How did you find that out?" Zeke asked.

"June Bug telegraphed me," Hassa replied. "He was worried about you getting on my bad side."

Zeke let out a breath. "Give me an address and he's good as caught."

Hassa reached into his jacket then extracted a folded piece of paper. He handed it to Zeke.

"His name is Clyde Blanchet. This is his tintype. You'll find him residing at the address on the back of the image. You can bring him back alive or dead. It doesn't matter to me."

"It matters to me," Zeke said. "If he ain't broke no laws, I'll try my best not to shoot."

Hassa shrugged. "It's your choice."

"You got plenty of men at your disposal," Zeke said. "Why not send them?"

"My men are guards," Hassa replied. "They can handle a drunken socialite or two, but Clyde Blanchet is pretty good with a gun. I need a professional. Besides, our people are not welcomed."

Zeke folded the paper then stuck it in his pocket.

"Give me a couple of days."

"That's all?" Hassa looked skeptical.

"I'm in a hurry," Zeke said. "You'll have your man by sundown tomorrow."

Zeke hurried back to his steam car then began to journey to Macon, thankful that June Bug intervened. He arrived at the edge of town a few minutes past midnight. All the hotels were long shut down, so Zeke found a nice spot behind a large red tip bush, parked, and then settled in for a night's sleep in his car. The morning sun was his alarm, its warmth and intensity forcing open his weary eyelids. He started the steam car then drove into the city. Macon was the largest metropolis in central Georgia but nowhere near as sophisticated as Atlanta. The steam car caused a commotion as more than a few horses reared and threw riders at its passing while children and some adults gawked and pointed. Zeke parked in front of the nearest restaurant, an establishment with the name Bertha's hanging over its doors. As he walked inside, he was greeted by a tall stout woman with gray-streaked black hair and a warm smile. A dingy apron covered her plain dress.

"Welcome to Bertha's!" the woman shouted. "You ain't from around here."

Zeke took off his hat then bowed. "No, I'm not."

"I know everyone in Macon and the surrounding three counties. What's your name, stranger?"

"Zeke Culpepper. Pleased to meet you. You must be Bertha."

"That I am," Bertha said. "Now that we've dispensed with the pleasantries, find yourself a seat and Bertha here will feed you. What do you want?"

"What do you have?"

"Anything meant to be eaten for breakfast and a few things that weren't."

"I'm a simple man," Zeke said. "Fix me up some grits, scrambled eggs and bacon. And if you have it, I'd like a glass of orange juice and black coffee.

"Your food will be right out," Bertha answered. "Best breakfast in Georgia coming right up!

Bertha wasn't boasting. Zeke wasn't sure if it was the best breakfast in Georgia, but it was sure the best breakfast he'd enjoyed in a spell. He was finishing his eggs when he felt a hard thump on his shoulder. He turned to look into the face of a disgruntled policeman. The red-faced officer glared at him then spoke through his voluminous moustache.

"That your automobile outside?" the officer asked.

"Yes, it is," Zeke replied.

"I'm going to have to ask you to remove it from city limits. That damn thing is scaring the hell out of the horses."

"I'll do that right away, sir, but I believe I'll scare as many on the way out as I did on the way in. How about me leaving it right where it is until I'm on my way, which will probably be tonight."

The policeman tipped his cap with his Billy club.

"That makes sense," he said. "What's your name?"

Zeke wiped his hands with his napkin the stood. He and the officer shook hands.

"Zeke Culpepper."

"Please to meet you, Mr. Culpepper. I'm Officer Graddick. Where are you staying?"

"Nowhere right now. I'm looking for this place."

Zeke handed Graddick Hassa Ola's note.

"The Magnolia Hotel," he said. "It's a few blocks south of here, down the hill and by the river. It's a nice place."

"Thank you, officer," Zeke said. "I'll head that way as soon as I'm done with this here delicious breakfast."

"Best breakfast in Georgia," the officer said.

He tipped his hat then headed for the door.

"Stay out of trouble, Mr. Culpepper," he said.

"That's the plan, Officer."

Zeke finished his breakfast then took a stroll to the Magnolia Hotel, studying the route as he made his way to the river. The hotel was fine structure, about three stories high with wide white columns flanking the entrance and a front porch lined with white rocking chairs. A few of the residents indulged themselves despite the chilly air, waving at passersby and giving Zeke a friendly nod. He studied each one as he climbed the stairs; none matched the tintype tucked in his pocket.

A stocky brown-skinned man draped in a custom fit butler's uniform and shiny black top hat greeted him at the double door entrance.

"Welcome the Magnolia Hotel, the finest hotel in Freedonia!" he announced. "I'm Jefferson Davidson, the concierge. Are you visiting someone residing in our fine establishment or will you be taking a room?"

"I'll be staying, if there's room," Zeke said.

"Providence shines on you today," Jefferson said. "Some of my finest suites are available, and I can tell a man like you insists on only the best."

"I slept in my automobile last night," Zeke said. "I'm used to less."

Jefferson let out a boisterous laugh. "That's makes it even more important that your rest tonight is like sleeping in Heaven. Allow me to escort you to our check in desk."

Jefferson was beginning to get on Zeke's nerves despite his Christian patience. He nodded his head toward the desk.

"Is that it right there?" he asked.

"Yes, it is," Jefferson replied.

"I think I can make it on my own."

"I insist!" Jefferson said. "I can inform you about the amazing amenities of our hotel and this enchanting city."

Zeke shrugged. "Lead the way."

He tuned out Jefferson's exposition as he studied the lobby. A spiral staircase climbed to the third floor, more show than practical. A circular couch rested beside the staircase; two gaily dressed woman sat there deep in an apparently interesting conversation. They halted, raising their eyes to study Zeke and share sweet smiles. One of the women leaned close to the other then spoke in a language that surprised Zeke.

"Oh oh. Gade kisa fet mache la. Tonnerre, bèl ti mesye li ye, wi. Gade,Fabiola! Gade nan!"

The other woman gave her friend a stern look.

"Ay! Kenbe tèt ou sou ki sa n'ap fè la. Nou ka pale avec li pita. Ou séch, Stephanie, ou konnen sa?"

Zeke grinned then tipped his hat.

"Mesi, madam, pou bèl konpleman. Bèl jou-nen."

The women gasped then laughed. Zeke winked, and then continued to the check in desk.

A blond-haired woman with a powdered face, glaring red lips and welcoming smile stood behind the check in desk. She was about to open her mouth to speak when a gruff voice filled the lobby.

"How hard is it to make eggs over easy?" the male voice shouted. "I've been in this hotel for weeks and that imbecile of a cook hasn't got it right yet!"

The lobby rang with the sound of breaking glass. Jefferson lowered his head, worrying his brow with his fingers.

"Excuse the altercation," he said. "Some of our guests are harder to please than others. Mr. Blanchet is such a guest."

Zeke's eyebrows rose. He looked up to see an upset maid hurrying down the third-floor corridor to the staircase. A ruddy faced man with black hair and a handlebar moustache pursued her.

"I pay too much money for this shoddy service," he yelled. He glared down into the lobby, his eyes lingering on Zeke.

"What the hell are y'all looking at?" he stomped back down the hallway.

"That was easy," Zeke whispered.

The blond woman grinned at Zeke, keeping her professional demeanor despite Blanchet's behavior.

"Welcome to the Magnolia," she sang. "I apologize for the disturbance. Mr. Blanchet is a very demanding customer."

"I see," Zeke said. "I promise to be a little quieter."

"Any preference?" she asked.

"As long as the room has a bed, I'm fine," Zeke replied.

"I'll put you on the first floor. The rooms are a bit larger and you'll be closer to the kitchen."

"Excellent choice!" Jefferson announced.

Zeke looked at the concierge, fighting not to roll his eyes. The woman gave him his keys.

"Enjoy your stay, Mr. Culpepper."

"Follow me please," Jefferson said.

Zeke was walking behind the annoying man when he heard a sweet voice call out.

"Sir?"

He turned to see one of the Haitian ladies approaching, the one who thought he was handsome.

"Pardon my interruption," she said. "My name is Stephanie Alcimbert."

She extended her hand. Zeke took her hand then kissed it.

"Ezekiel Culpepper," he said.

"I'm shocked," she said. "I thought you were Haitian. Your Creole is perfect."

"The little I know. I served in the New Haitian Army for a time. Picked up a few words here and there."

"My sister Fabiola and I would love to have dinner with you," she said.

"Thanks for the offer, Stephanie, but I'm here on serious business which doesn't allow any time for socializing."

Stephanie pouted. "You break my heart. But I understand. We are here on business as well."

Zeke kissed Stephanie's hand once more.

"It was nice meeting you," he said. "Have a wonderful evening."

"You too, Ezekiel Culpepper."

Stephanie strolled away, giving Zeke a parting glance.

"Not a smart decision I would say," Jefferson commented.

"It's none of your business," Zeke replied.

He followed the concierge to his room. It was a quant space with a small bed and a porcelain wash basin, a nice for a town like Macon, but nowhere near the luxury the hotel advertised. It didn't matter; he didn't plan to stay long. He tipped Jefferson, quickly undressed then took a well-deserved nap.

When Zeke finally woke it was dusk. He took his time dressing then rang the bell for a maid to bring warm water for his basin. There was a light knock on his door. When he opened it, he realized his luck was still good. The woman bringing his water was the same woman Blanchet chased from his room.

"Welcome to the Magnolia," she said. She slipped by Zeke to fill his basin.

"That was quite a scene earlier," he said.

The woman turned to look at him with wide eyes.

"You saw that?"

Zeke nodded.

"I was so embarrassed!" she said. "I hate Mr. Blanchet!"

"How long has he been here?" Zeke asked.

"Too long! Almost three weeks!"

"Does he stay in his room all the time?"

The maid shook her head. "No. He goes to the saloon every evening, then returns around midnight. I hear he gambles all the time."

Zeke grinned. Old habits die hard. "Does he win?"

"Yes and no," she said. "I heard he's really not that good. It's just everyone is scared to lose to him. The rumor is he's a gunslinger on the run."

"Is that so?"

The maid took on a worried look.

"Excuse me, mister. Why are you asking all these questions? I don't want no trouble."

"You're fine, miss," Zeke said. "Just curious, that's all."

"Are you a marshal or something? Is Mr. Blanchet in trouble?"

"Like I said, just curious. Thank you for the fresh water."

The maid smiled at him nervously. "You're welcome."

She opened the door to leave then turned to him.

"I hope you are here to get him sir," she said. "I hope you kill him."

"Goodbye ma'am," Zeke said.

He closed the door behind her.

"I hope it won't come to that."

Zeke lingered close to his room, cleaning his weapons and observing the ins and outs of the hotel. He was in the lobby when Blanchet left his room, walking down the stairs in a finely tailored suit and a leather derby. Again their eyes met as Blanchet passed by. Zeke nodded; Blanchet returned the nod then exited the hotel. A few moments later the two lovely ladies Zeke met earlier left the hotel as well. Stephanie exchanged smiles with him; Fabiola smirked then winked. Stephanie reminded him of Pauline and a somber mood took hold. He had to find her; he also had to discover why she was taken. He hadn't had much time to think about the circumstances and the information shared; all he knew was that some Cuban officials apprehended her and he was going to get her back.

Zeke returned to his room. He lay on his bed, and then dozed off. His alarm woke him at 11:30 pm. He strapped on his guns, kissed his cross then tucked it in his shirt, opened his door then went down into the empty lobby. He positioned himself in front of the spiral staircase then pushed back his jacket so his shotgun would be easy to reach. At exactly midnight, Blanchet strode through the door. Zeke stood then tipped his hat.

"Welcome back, Mr. Blanchet," Zeke said. "I've been waiting for you. We have business to attend to."

"Wait just a cotton-picking minute!" A female voice called out.

The Haitian ladies strode through the door, the pleasant smiles gone from their faces. Each held Winchesters in their gloved hands, Fabiola aiming at Zeke, Stephanie aiming at Blanchet.

"I told you we should have taken him yesterday," Fabiola said.

"Hush up, Fabiola!" Stephanie replied. "It doesn't make any difference now. We got the drop on both of them."

Zeke would have normally agreed. Bounty hunter rule number one? First to draw claimed the bounty. But Blanchet was his ticket to kerosene and Pauline.

"I'm afraid I'm going to have to dispute your claim," he said.

Fabiola shook her head. "You can't. You know the law."

"It's not a real law," Zeke said.

"The hell with this!" Blanchet exclaimed. "I ain't going with nobody!"

Blanchet snatched out his revolvers and began shooting, nicking Zeke's shoulder. Fabiola spun to the floor holding her gut. Stephanie worked her lever action in a blur, the Winchester sounding like a Gatling gun as she made her way to her wounded sister.

Zeke chased Blanchet as he sprinted toward the rear of the hotel. He shot ahead of the running gambler, cutting him off with buckshot. Blanchet almost fell trying to avoid the flying lead. He leaped onto the staircase, shooting as he climbed. His shots were accurate; each one whizzed close to Zeke, forcing him to seek cover. Stephanie did the same, tucking her rifle under her arm, and then dragging her sister behind a lobby sofa.

Blanchet reached the second floor. He disappeared down the hallway.

"He's going out the window!" Stephanie shouted.

"I wish he would," Zeke said. "All we'd have to do then is fight over his dead body."

Fabiola moaned. Stephanie stroked her cheek, and then kissed her on the forehead.

"Hang in there, sister," she whispered. "This will be over in a while."

Zeke studied the wounded woman then rubbed his cross through his shirt. That was a bad gut wound; if they didn't get Fabiola to a doctor soon, she would die.

"Look Stephanie," he said. "Slide that rifle over to me. I'll lay down cover fire while you and your sister skedaddle."

Stephanie's eyes narrowed. "You're trying to take our bounty!"

"You got a choice," he said. "Your sister or this bounty."

"Don't do it," Fabiola said. "I'll be fine. We need the money."

"I need you more," Stephanie said. She slid Fabiola's rifle to Zeke. He scooped up the gun, taking a moment to admire the craftsmanship and balance before checking how many rounds he had to work with.

"Go," he said.

Zeke sprang from behind his cover, shooting the Winchester as fast as he could. Stephanie wrapped one arm around Fabiola's waist then dragged her toward the door, firing her rifle with one hand.

Blanchet managed to get off a few shots, grazing Stephanie's shoulder and nicking Zeke's left thigh. Zeke fell back behind cover and then checked his wound.

"Damn he's good," he whispered. "Gonna be hard collecting this payday without killing this . . . child of God."

Stephanie and Fabiola made it out of the hotel. Zeke settled behind a large lounge chair while he reloaded. He decided he'd try a little verbal persuasion.

"There's only four ways you're getting out of here, Clyde!" Zeke shouted. "A bullet in your head, a bullet in your heart, or a bullet in your ass. And don't think that bullet in your ass can't kill you."

"What's the fourth way?" Clyde shouted back.

"You give me that money you owe Hassa Ola. I figure he'll be happy with that for a while. It'll give you time to get your things in order and get the hell out of Macon."

"Them ladies ain't going to just let me walk away!" Clyde shouted.

"I'll deal with them," Zeke said. "You just come on down so we don't have to kill each other."

"Okay. I'll take the fourth way," Clyde shouted.

"I thought you would," Zeke shouted back. "Toss your pieces down the stairs one by one."

Zeke stepped from behind the lounge chair. A Colt tumbled down the stairs. Zeke frowned.

"I'm going to need you to throw them all down here, Clyde."

"Gonna have to bring that last one down with me," Clyde called back. "I'm kind of attached to it."

Zeke braced his shotgun against his shoulder, taking aim at the top of the stairs.

"Come on down then," he said.

Clyde emerged from the darkness; his arms raised high. His left arm immediately caught Zeke's attention. A black revolver extended from the end of arm attached directly to his wrist.

"I'll be damned," Zeke whispered.

Blanchet smiled as he came closer, extending his right hand. Zeke lowered his shotgun and they shook.

"I recognize you now," Clyde said. "You're Zeke Culpepper. I should have known."

"Good to meet you, Clyde," Zeke said. "Wish it was under better circumstances."

Clyde shrugged. "I'm just glad to be alive now that I know who was after me. If I hadn't run out of bullets, things might be different."

"Won't disagree with you there," Zeke said. He reached into his shirt then took out his cross. Clyde laughed.

"So, it is true," he said. "You are a preacher!"

"I'm a deacon," Zeke corrected, "and I ain't got much time. Let's get up to your room and get that money."

Zeke followed Clyde up the stairs. Hotel guests peeked out their rooms as the two walked by; others gathered in the lobby talking excitedly about the gun battle. Luckily no one else was hurt from all the flying bullets. Clyde handed Zeke the key to his room and Zeke reached around the gunslinger, opening the door. Clyde's room was neat and orderly. He was apparently planning on leaving the next day for his bags were packed and placed against the wall.

"I knew something was up," Clyde said. "I noticed you the day you checked in. Didn't spot those ladies though."

"You should have gone with your instincts," Zeke said.

"Yeah, I should have."

Clyde pointed to a small blue carpet bag. "Hassa Ola's money is in there plus a little extra. You can keep it."

Zeke picked up the bag, and then placed it on the bed. He opened it then whistled.

"That's a lot of money," he said.

"It's all there," Clyde replied.

Zeke closed the bag.

"I guess that concludes our business."

Stephanie burst through the door, her Winchester braced on her hip. The rifle blared and blood bloomed on Clyde's leg. The gambler rolled to the floor drawing his limbs close and tight as he could. Stephanie turned the gun on Zeke.

"I knew it!You're working with him!"

Zeke raised his hands.

"Now wait just a minute," he said. "I ain't doing no such thing."

"You're a damned liar!" she shouted.

Zeke rolled his eyes. "I ain't got time for this!"

He pivoted to his left, taking himself out of the line of fire while simultaneously grabbing the

Winchester barrel. Stephanie fired; Zeke grimaced from the heat as he snatched the gun from Stephanie's grip. He struck her on the head with the gun butt. Stephanie collapsed to the floor dazed.

"I got places to be," he said. "I made a deal with Clyde; give me the money and I'd let him go. I was going to cut you and your sister in on the ransom."

"I'll get more taking him back to New Haiti," Stephanie said as she rubbed her head.

"Take him, then," Zeke said. "I'd normally disagree with you, but he gave Fabiola a bad gut wound. Besides, I don't owe the man anything. I'm done here. I hope your sister is okay."

Zeke looked at Clyde who lay on the floor grimacing.

"Sorry about this," Zeke said.

"Go to Hell, Zeke Culpepper!" Clyde barked.

Zeke hurried out the room to the stairs, carpet bag in hand. The lobby overflowed with guests and the curious, their chatter filling his ears. As he descended the spiral staircase, he spotted the officer he had a run in with earlier. This time Jefferson had three friends with him and none of them were smiling. The officer met him at the base of the stairs, his hand on the revolver at his waist.

"I should have known you had something to do with this!" he said. "You had trouble written all over your face."

"I'm here on a legal bounty hunt," Zeke replied. "That man upstairs owed my client money. If you'll allow me, I can show you my credentials."

Zeke leaned over slowly, placing the bag on the floor. He reached into his inside jacket pocket, took out his bounty hunter license, and then handed it to Jefferson.

The officer pushed the papers back to Zeke. "I don't need to see your damn papers! You endangered the lives of innocent people. Somebody could have been killed!"

"Nobody was," Zeke answered. "So, unless you're going to try to arrest me, I suggest you let me be on my way."

Zeke put an emphasis on the word 'try.' He rested his hands on his hip near his shotgun stock. Jefferson's expression transformed from anger to worry.

"Besides, I don't think you want Hassa Ola to know you interfered with his business," Zeke added.

The officers shifted about as if a sudden itch had overcome them. All four stepped aside.

"Get out of here," Jefferson said, attempting to regain some authority in his voice. "And stay the hell out of Macon!"

"That's the plan," Zeke said. He tipped his hat to the officers, and then strolled out of the hotel.

Zeke fast-walked to his steam car then drove to the Casino. The building still glowed with the lights of activity despite the late hour. This time his meeting with the guards was more amicable.

"I'm here to see Hassa Ola," he said.

One of the guards went inside then returned moments later with Hassa. Hassa's smile disappeared when he saw Zeke was alone.

"Where's Blanchet?" he asked.

"In Macon," Zeke replied. "I brought you this, though."

Zeke took the carpet bag from the car.

Hassa motioned with his head and his guards collected the bag. They opened it for their boss, who knelt down then counted the contents. A smile formed on his face.

"It's all here and then some," Hassa Ola said. "But I wanted Blanchet, too."

"You're not going to get him," Zeke said. "But he ain't getting away. There were two other bounty hunters looking for him from New Haiti. They got him; you got the money. Now where's my kerosene?"

"This is not the deal we struck, Culpepper," Hassa said. "I'll give you a pass since we just met and you didn't know better. The kerosene is out back. Two wagons full."

Zeke followed Hassa and the guards to the rear of the casino. A wide smile broke on his face when he saw the wagons filled with metal kerosene barrels hitched to four stout mules. The drivers stood between the wagons engaged in small talk.

"I guess our business is done," Zeke said.

"Wait a minute," Hassa Ola said. "You ain't planning on leaving tonight, are you?"

"I sure am. I figure if we leave now, we'll get to June Bug's about daybreak. We'll fill up that dragonfly and be on our way to Savannah about noon."

"Damn," Hassa Ola said. "You love that woman, don't you?"

Zeke pushed back his hand. "I reckon I do."

He shook Hassa's hand.

"Tell your boys to follow me," Zeke said. "I got headlamps on my car. It'll be slow going, but we'll get there."

"You heard the man," Hassa said to the drivers. "Line up behind him and stay close."

Hassa winked at Zeke. "Goodbye, Zeke Culpepper, and good luck."

Zeke took his cross from inside his shirt.

"Luck ain't got nothing to do with it."

He started his car, turned on the headlamps then headed down the road to June Bug's farm, the wagons close behind.

- 8 -

Salvador Abrantes's defunct plantation languished on the edge of a mango swamp, a collection of dilapidated buildings and neglected sugar cane fields. Twenty years ago, the plantation thrived, reaping the benefits of the sugar business that migrated to Cuba and other islands after the Haitian Revolution.

Pauline gazed upon the master's mansion, a bitter taste swelling in her mouth. This was what she'd fought against, something her comrades continued to fight long after she escaped. She studied their faces; none of them seemed resentful or angry.

She remembered the day she fled to Freedonia. The New Spanish army landed in Havana thirty days prior and began a campaign which bordered on genocide. The rebel planters, fearing the destruction of their livelihood capitulated, leaving the rebel army with little support. A meeting was called among the rebel leaders, a meeting she remembered well. Although Pauline, Maceo and the others wished to continue the fight, the wisdom of Juarez overruled their energy. Word came from the Spaniards that the leaders would be allowed to leave peacefully if they refused to fight any further. If they did not, Cuba would become a killing ground. They all knew that no matter where they chose to go

New Spain would one day come for them. The choice was clear; stay and risk the death of everyone she knew and loved, or leave and take her chances on the run. She and the other leaders chose to leave. Maceo and Gomez traveled throughout the Caribbean and South America attempting to gain allies and raise support for the revival of the revolution, their lives under constant threat from New Spain assassins. Pauline did the opposite, finding peace and refuge in Freedonia.

The wagons rolled by the mansion to the section that had once been the slave quarters. A chill swept her; she never liked these spaces. If it was up to her every one of them would be burned to the ground. Others felt a bond to the tiny abodes, claiming them to be heritage and a symbol of perseverance and survival. To Pauline they were blights of a past best left behind.

The wagons halted under a huge oak tree, an ancestor tree as they were once called. Pauline climbed out the wagon then followed the others to the base of the ancient tree. An elderly man with stark white hair that contrasted with his black skin shuffled to the center of the group. A woman approximately the same age accompanied him, her hair covered with a multi-colored wrap. The man and woman shared warm smiles with Pauline.

"This is truly a special day," the man said. "The ancestors have finally brought our daughter home!"

"Ase!" everyone exclaimed.

The woman stepped forward, her arms extended. "We thought we lost you, Paulina."

Pauline went to the woman and they hugged.

'I was lost, mama," she said. Corinne was not her true mother, but everyone addressed her so.

Her mother Carmen died two years after Pauline left for Freedonia. She had not been able to attend her funeral, another wound inflicted by New Spain.

Pauline stepped away from Corinne and Diego to face everyone.

"I must tell you this before we move forward so that any decisions you make are based on the truth. I did not come back on my own accord. I was discovered by Cuban authorities who took me from Freedonia intending to try me for my so-called crimes. If they had not taken me . . ."

"You would have found another way to come home."

Pauline didn't recognize the man who spoke. He stepped forward and the others looked at him with familiarity and respect. The umber-skinned man was extremely tall and broad shouldered. He was bald, the scars on his cheeks deliberate. Small golden earrings glimmered with the firelight; when he smiled Pauline felt at ease.

Diego shuffled to the man then took his arm, leading him to Pauline.

"Daughter, this is Dominic Valdez," Diego said.

Dominic dropped to one knee then took Pauline's hand, surprising her.

"La Rosa de Matanzas," he said. "It is an honor to meet you. It is rare that one finds oneself before the reincarnation of the ancestors."

"I don't know what you mean," Pauline replied.

Dominic stood. "The spirit of Carlota resides in you. I can feel her presence."

"I would not dare claim to be so blessed," Pauline said.

"Dominic has led us for the past five years," Diego said. "It was he who planned your rescue."

Pauline's eyes narrowed. "Then Dominic and I have much to discuss."

Dominic grinned. "Yes, we do. But not now. We will celebrate your return then we will talk of other matters."

Pauline nodded.

Drummers and dancers emerged from the darkness, forming a larger circle before the ancestor tree around the bonfire. Silence was dispelled by their vigorous beat, a rhythm from her homeland of Matanzas. Pauline was pensive at first, watching the others sing and dance while she processed the events of the previous days. Someone blocked the flickering light from the bonfire; Pauline looked up into Dominic's smiling face.

"Dance with me," he said.

"It's been a long time," Pauline replied.

"Which is why you should," he said. "The people have accepted me as one of their leaders, but before me there were you, Maceo and the others. It will be good for them to see that we are unified, even if we are not. At least not yet."

He grinned as he offered his hand. Pauline smirked, and then took Dominic's hand. She gasped as he lifted her to her feet.

"I warn you, I'm not the best dancer," she said.

"But I am," Dominic replied. "I will make us both look good."

Pauline followed Dominic into the circle and the others cheered. The drummers increased the pace and they danced. Pauline quickly remembered the steps to the secret dance, keeping pace with

Dominic. He didn't lie; he was an excellent dancer, lithe and athletic.

"You lied," Dominic said as they danced.

"Lied about what?" Pauline replied.

"You are a good dancer," he said.

"Not as good as you."

Dominic laughed. "Very few are."

Pauline was winded much sooner than she expected. She stopped, raising her hands in surrender and the others moaned playfully in response. Dominic didn't seem to notice. His attention was captured by something behind her. She turned to see a man waving in the distance, near the dilapidated master's house. Dominic strode by her.

"Come with me," he said. "It's time for our meeting."

Pauline followed Dominic to the mysterious man. The man took off his hat, and then bowed.

"La Rosa," he said. "It is an honor to meet you."

"Who are you?" Pauline asked.

"I am Hernando Gomez," he answered.

"Hernando is our contact to our Freedonian friends," Dominic said.

"Contact to Freedonia?" A tight frown formed on Pauline's face."What the hell is going on here?"

"If you would follow me please," Hernando asked.

Pauline did not move, her eyes shifting between the two men. She was sure she could take Hernando, but Dominic might prove to be difficult. Fighting the two of them at the same time would probably prove impossible, but she would not go back to the Spaniards without a struggle. She braced herself, but neither man seemed ready to use force against here.

"Please La Rosa," Hernando said. "We mean you no harm."

"He's right," Dominic said. "Please trust us."

Pauline finally nodded her approval. They walked to the rear of the house, eventually reaching another clearing where a small fire burned. A man sat before the flames, smoking a cigar. Although he was dressed as Cuban, he was obviously not. He took the cigar from his lips, and then smiled.

"Pauline Rose," he said. "We finally meet face to face."

Hernando sat beside the man. Pauline and Dominic remained standing.

"I'm John Scobel," the man said. "I represent Freedonia in this manner."

"John Scobel," Pauline repeated. "Head of Field Operations for the Freedonia Dispatches."

John smiled. "You've done your homework."

"I've heard your name around."

"Probably from your boyfriend, Ezekiel Culpepper."

Hearing Zeke's name angered her.

"I don't like people in my business, Mr. Scobel. Why did Freedonia sell me out? Why am I here?"

"You're correct. We did inform the Cubans of your whereabouts," he confessed. "We needed you back here for our own purposes."

"A Gullah woman is dead because of your purposes," Pauline said.

"That is as much your fault as ours," Scobel replied. "If you had only cooperated Mary would still be alive. We didn't expect your resistance to be so . . . vigorous."

"That's exactly what Gonzales said," Pauline said.

Scobel stood.

"I can assure you that Gonzales and I are not on the same side. We wanted you here for our own reason."

Pauline folded her arms. "Which is?"

Scobel took a puff of his cigar. "Officially New Spain and Freedonia are diplomatic allies. Unofficially we are fighting for control of the Southern Atlantic and the Caribbean Sea. Add to that the fact that New Spain and New Haiti are enemies you can see that our relationship is delicate."

"This still doesn't explain why I am here," she said.

"We received information that New Spain is building a warship that could tip the balance of our oceanic standoff. The Freedonian Navy has dominated the region for twenty years. We're not about to lose our position now. Since we are technically allies, we can't move against Cuba without involving New Spain. So, we needed home grown opposition to fulfill our agenda."

Pauline gave Dominic the side eye. "Who exactly are you fighting for?"

"I could care less about Freedonia or its concerns," Dominic answered. "But the revolution is weak. Ever since you and the others escaped, we have been in disarray. Freedonia has promised us support if we help them locate this warship and destroy it."

"I still don't see why I'm here," Pauline said. "There are better leaders to rally our fighters. Maceo or Gomez would have been better choices."

"Both men are too visible for now," Scobel said. "Because the two of them parade around the

Caribbean seeking support for their return New Spain keeps a close eye on them. But you managed to disappear. Besides, your following is much stronger than you know, or than you'll admit."

Pauline's hands fell to her hips. "Again, why am I here?"

"The revolt is not organized enough to defeat the local Spaniards and their allies," Scobel said. "The planters are weak as well. Many of them will not take up arms and join with the workers and the enslaved. There was a time when all three fought together under one leadership."

The men looked at Pauline. She frowned as she realized what they wanted from her.

"That was a long time ago," she said.

"Your father is still well-respected among the planters," Dominic said.

"I haven't spoken to my father in ten years," Pauline replied.

"It's time you did," Scobel said.

"Look, I didn't agree to any of this," Pauline replied. "I'm here . . ."

"Against your will?" Scobel took another puff of his cigar. "I'm sure all those people out there celebrating your return would love to hear you say that."

She looked at Dominic. The big man stared at her with his arms folded across his chest, his face grim.

"I would have come if asked," she said. "There was no need for this ruse."

"How you arrived doesn't matter now. You're here," Scobel said. "You now have the perfect opportunity to help your people and Freedonia."

Pauline looked at Dominic. "Does my father still live at the plantation?"

Dominic shook his head. "He lives in Havana now."

"That makes things more difficult."

"Difficult but not impossible," Scobel replied. "Let me handle it."

"No," Pauline said. "I'll do it my way. The less from you, the better."

Scobel grinned. "Either way I get what I want."

There was someone else Pauline needed to visit, but that information she would keep to herself.

Scobel puffed his cigar then smiled. "Hernandez will join your group. He's my contact. If you need anything from us, he can make it available. Once you've met your father and made amends with the planters, I can reveal to you the rest of our plan."

"And if I can't get the planters' approval?" Pauline asked.

"Then we'll have to pursue an alternative route and the rebels will receive nothing from Freedonia," Scobel said.

Scobel tipped his hat. "Good luck, La Rosa. A lot of people are depending on you."

Scobel strolled away into the darkness, followed by Hernandez. Dominic touched Pauline's shoulder and she flinched.

"He's right," he said. "The people see you as their victory."

The two were silent as they returned to the celebration. Although she was angry about the method, she was glad to be home. Seeing old friends and comrades has stirred emotions she thought long dead. There was still a fight and the people were willing. But was she the right choice?

"I've been gone too long," Pauline said. "My life in Freedonia was peaceful. I'm not the woman I used to be."

"Tell me one thing," Dominic said. "Are you willing to try?"

Pauline looked at the workers, their celebration still full and joyous.

"Yes," she said. "Let's get back to the celebration. Our friends may get the wrong idea."

Dominic grinned. "That wouldn't be so bad. They would think we are closer."

She glared at Dominic. "It would be for me. Let's go."

As they walked back to the bonfire Pauline thought of Zeke. She would do what she had to do, and then she would return to Freedonia. That was her home now. At least that was what she told herself.

- 9 -

June Bug stood in his front yard wiping his hands with a rag as if he had anticipated Zeke's return. Zeke cruised up the dirt road; the kerosene laden wagons close behind. June Bug walked up to him as he climbed out his car.

"I'll be damned," he said. "You pulled it off."

"Yep," Zeke replied. "How soon before we can get airborne?"

"Don't you want to rest?" June Bug asked. "You been driving all night I suspect."

"Yes, we have!" one of the wagoneers yelled out.

Zeke shook his head. "Every minute that passes Pauline's trail gets colder. The sooner we get on the better."

"Zeke Culpepper shut your mouth!"

Ceely shoved the screen door aside then stomped across the front porch, down the stairs then right up to Zeke, their noses almost touching.

"If I wasn't a Godly woman, I'd whoop your hide from here to Atlanta," she said between her teeth. "I don't know what you done got my man into, but whatever it is he ain't leaving on an empty stomach!"

Ceely peered around Zeke at the wagon drivers.

"Y'all get them wagons around back then come in and wash up for breakfast."

The men tipped their hats, climbed onto the wagons then guided them behind the house.

"You two follow me," she said. "And no sassing, Ezekiel Culpepper."

Zeke, June Bug, the wagon drivers and the children all sat down to a big breakfast of grits, biscuits, scrambled eggs, and sausage. Despite his impatience, Zeke was glad for the meal. He shoveled his food down, and then stood as he wiped his mouth.

"That was great, Ceely," he said. "Now can we get to moving around here?"

June Bug pushed his plate away. "That was mighty fine, baby. Come on, Zeke. Let's get his bird in the air."

Ceely took their plates. "The way you rushing I'd think you got some things you need to do too, June Bug."

"I'm just helping out a friend, honey pie," he answered. "And the sooner I get him where he needs to be, the sooner I can get back to you."

"Get out of here with your lying self," Ceely said. "And bring me back some shrimp!"

Zeke followed June Bug to the barn where he kept the dragonfly. They pushed the doors open then took a few of the kerosene canisters from the wagons.

"Looks like just enough," June Bug said.

"I think it's more than enough," Zeke replied.

"It would be if I was planning on landing and refueling."

June Bug shared a mischievous smile with Zeke.

"What you done did, boy?" Zeke asked.

"Look a here." June Bug stepped into a shadowy corner of the barn then emerged with two oval shaped metal canisters, one tucked under each arm.

"What are those?" Zeke asked.

June Bug grinned wider. "I call 'em cheaters. Come on give me a hand."

Zeke grabbed one of the canisters and was abruptly reminded of June bug's strength. He began falling then let go as he stumbled forward, jumping over the canister then catching himself before crashing face first into the hay.

"Hey!" June bug shouted. "Be careful."

Zeke rolled the canister to the dragonfly.

"There's a twist lid on the top," June bug said. "Open it up then fill it with kerosene."

Zeke located the cap then did as June bug instructed. June Bug came to his side of the craft then slid open a brass panel, revealing two latches and an open port. He lifted the filled canister then attached it to the craft.

"Extra fuel for longer distances?" Zeke asked.

"You got it," June Bug replied. "These puppies help me fly back and forth a ways without refueling. Saves me money and time."

"Now why would you be in a situation where you'd need to be so discreet?"

"Built these a long time ago. You see they're dusty."

"Ain't the extra weight going to slow us down?" Zeke asked.

"I modified the engine to handle the weight. We'll lose a little speed but not much. Besides, I have a little doo-hickey in my cockpit that allows me drop the cheaters if I get in a tight spot."

"But you haven't had to do that in a while, huh?" Zeke asked.

"No sir," June Bug replied.

The wagon drivers wandered into the barn, rubbing their stomachs and smiling.

"Y'all come over here and help roll *Paw-Paw* outside," June Bug said.

Zeke eyebrows rose. "*Paw-Paw*?"

"Yep. Named it after my granddaddy."

"Your granddaddy probably had a real name."

"I'm sure he did, but he never let us grand-kids use it. Said it was disrespectful."

The men rolled the dragonfly out of the barn to the middle of a nearby fallow field. The children gathered about, clapping their hands and laughing as the men positioned the craft for takeoff. Ceely brought Zeke and June Bug caps and heavy leather jackets. The jacket fit big on Zeke but he wouldn't dare take it off. The higher they flew, the colder it would get. Once he buttoned up the jacket he trotted to his car, and then retrieved his traveling bag. He gave the bag to June Bug who stored it in the cargo hold. Ceely gave June Bug a kiss and Zeke a stern stare.

"Don't you get my man in trouble, Ezekiel Culpepper," she said.

She is really upset with me, Zeke thought. *She keeps using my full name.*

"I promise I won't," Zeke said as he tipped his hat. "Let's get this show on the road!"

June Bug climbed into the forward cockpit. Zeke spun the left propeller, then the right. The children cheered as *Paw-Paw* roared to life.

"Bye Daddy!" they shouted.

Zeke climbed into the passenger cockpit. He snuggled in then put on his goggles.

"How long you expect this to take?" he shouted over the engine drone.

"With the wind behind us, about three hours," June Bug shouted back.

Zeke checked his pocket watch. "That's about 11:30 a.m."

"Yes sir!" June Bug replied. "Let's go!"

June Bug pulled back the lift lever and the propellers tilted upward. He pressed the accelerator and Paw-Paw lifted from the ground, rising slowly over the farm. Once they cleared the pines and red oaks, June Bug pushed the lift lever downward and the propellers tilted back to their original position. Paw-Paw lurched forward, cruising faster and faster until they barreled full speed to the east.

"Hold on, Pauline," Zeke whispered. *"I'm on my way!"*

They sped over the rolling piedmont then crossed the natural sand hills boundary into the flatlands. Zeke tried not to worry but Mary's words unsettled his thoughts. He'd knownPauline for three years. They flirted for a time before getting serious about their feelings. Now he felt like he had been with a stranger. They'd have a lot to talk about once he found her. He wasn't about to give up on her because of the lies. The woman he knew wasn't a total lie, of that he was sure.

"To your left!" June Bug shouted.

Zeke peered to his left. An object flew toward them, its details becoming clear as it approached.

"Another dragonfly," Zeke said aloud. "One of your friends?"

"Nope," June Bug said. "That's a government bug. Hang on!"

Paw-Paw jerked, clanked then pitched forward, rapidly picking up speed. Zeke looked over the side just in time to see the cheaters tumbling from the sky. He looked at the military dragonfly; it was still gaining on them.

"I think you need to fly a little faster," Zeke said.

"Can't," June Bug replied. "Too much weight."

"Well, I ain't planning on jumping out," Zeke said.

"They catch me with this bug and I'm going to jail," June Bug said.

"Maybe we can talk to him," Zeke replied.

June Bug laughed. "He'll shoot us down as soon as he's in range."

"Slow down, June Bug. We can't outrun him; we might as well try."

Paw-Paw slowed. Zeke raised his arms then waved his hands. The dragonfly eased alongside them. It was a single pilot craft, a sleek vehicle built for fighting. The pilot's face was hidden behind thick goggles and a leather cap.

"Can we help you?" Zeke said with a smile.

The man reached down into his cockpit then lifted a voice amplifier. He held the handle in his left hand then placed the round, compact speaker near his mouth. When he spoke, his voice boomed across the gap.

"Attention pilot! We have reason to believe Ezekiel Culpepper is accompanying you. He is wanted for questioning by the Freedonian Dispatches. Please follow me to Camp Stewart."

Zeke waved at the pilot and smiled.

"June Bug!" he shouted. "Can a dragonfly fly with one engine?"

"Yeah," June Bug shouted back. "It can't do vertical take-off or landing, but it . . . Zeke no!"

Zeke lifted his lever action shotgun and shot two rounds into the Freedonian pilot's engine. Sparks flew and fire flared as the pilot veered away.

"What the hell did you do that for?" June Bug shouted.

"Negotiations weren't working," Zeke said. "Besides, all those government flyboys have jump shutes. Put us down as soon as you can."

It didn't take June Bug long to find a clearing large enough to set Paw-Paw down. Zeke gathered his traveling bag, and then scrambled out.

"I'm in so much trouble," June Bug said.

Zeke ignored June Bug's lament.

"Let me see your map."

June Bug threw the map at Zeke. Zeke caught it; he spread it out on the fuselage then gave it a quick once over. According to his calculations they were a good day's ride from Savannah. He folded the map and handed it back to June Bug.

"Get on back home, June Bug," Zeke said calmly. "With me out you should be able to make better time. If they catch up with you, tell them I forced you to fly me here."

"But what about Paw-Paw?" June Bug fussed. "They're gonna confiscated him!"

"Once you show them some of the upgrades you've managed, they'll want to send you to Tuskegee."

June Bug scratched his head, a distant look on his face. "That wouldn't be so bad."

He looked at Zeke. "So, what are you gonna do? You're a wanted man."

"I'm going to walk to the nearest farm and steal a horse," Zeke said. "Then I'm going to ride to Savannah, get on the first boat to Cuba if have to, find Pauline then bring her back home."

"You make it sound so simple," June said.

"And you're wasting time," Zeke replied.

"Hold up now," June Bug said.

June Bug climbed out the cockpit. He ambled to the rear of the dragonfly and opened another compartment. He extracted a large case then opened it. Inside was a motorbike. He unfolded the bike, and then tightened a few bolts. He reached into the cargo hold again, taking out a small can of kerosene then filling the reservoir tank resting between the seat and the handlebars.

Zeke sat on the bike. "Well I'll be!"

"This will get you there a little faster," June Bug said. "The accelerator is on the right handle. Just twist it back toward you to go faster. This right here on the left grip is the brake. This little doodad by your left foot changes gears."

"You never cease to amaze me, June Bug," Zeke said as he patted his friend on the back.

June Bug knelt beside the motorbike then cranked it to a start. He detached the crank then handed it to Zeke.

"Good luck," he said. "I hope you find Pauline."

"I will," Zeke said. "Now get out of here."

Zeke watched June Bug climb into the cockpit, lift off then turn due west. He waved goodbye as Paw-Paw tilted then sped to the west.

Zeke shifted the bike into first gear, driving slowly over the rough field. So he was a wanted man. Hassa Ola most likely turned him in, payback for letting the man who owed him go. But Zeke couldn't do anything about that. He'd have to be more discreet in the future. He reached the paved road, shifted into second gear and sped toward Savannah.

-10-

Philippe Gonzales tapped his foot on the waxed wooden floor as he watched Governor Antonio Ramirez pour himself a glass of rum. He despised men like Ramirez, born to privilege and eager to flaunt their power whenever possible. It was the reason he'd spent the last hour sitting in the man's office as he handled 'more pressing matters,' as he said. It was merely a game to remind Gonzales who was in charge, an exercise apparently required in lieu of Philippe's recent debacle.

The governor took a sip of the rum then grinned.

"Mr. Barcardi delivered this rum to me personally," he said. "He claimed it was excellent. He was right. Have some?"

It was an offer meant to be refused.

"No thank you, Governor," Philippe said.

The governor finished his drink. He sat the glass on his desk then leaned back in his chair.

"I'm disappointed in you, Philippe. I sent you to Freedonia to perform a simple task and now I have a fugitive running free in my country."

"I apologize, Governor," Philippe said. "Apparently we were not the only ones informed of La Rosa's return."

"I know, and that vexes me," the governor replied. "Still, you would think that your best man would have been capable of keeping the woman in our custody."

Philippe had no response. He had been very disappointed in his men and shared his wrath days ago. The years of peace had made them soft. He would have to rectify that.

"Sir, may I propose a theory?" he said.

"Please do."

"I believe our Freedonian friends are playing both sides of the fence."

The governor leaned forward, placing his elbows on his desk as he intertwined his fingers.

"Explain."

"I believe La Rosa is here because the Freedonians want her here. They used us to deliver her then set up the raid on the passenger ship to free her."

"And what would they gain by it?"

"I don't know," Philippe confessed.

The governor leaned back in his chair. "I don't have time for theories. Our Excellency wants La Rosa captured, tried and hanged as soon as possible."

"Yes, Governor," Philippe replied.

The governor frowned. "You seem to have a problem with my orders."

Philippe silently cursed himself. He was never good at hiding his feelings.

"No, Governor. I'm merely thinking ahead. I apologize if I seem distracted."

The governor huffed. "Leave me. The next time I see you I expect to see La Rosa in your custody. Otherwise we'll have a more personal conversation."

Philippe stood, bowed then exited the room. He clinched his teeth as he strode down the corridor to the exit. That foppish bastard! Who was he to threaten anyone? It was people like Philippe who dirtied their hands in order for him to sit in his damn office and sip expensive rum.

He shook his head clear as he mounted his horse. Time to focus on immediate matters. There would be a change in Cuba one day, but it wouldn't be at the hands of a group of ragged workers led by a delusional woman. He was positive that Paulina's old friends were involved in her release. They were possibly hiding in the western forests, an area too dense and dangerous for him to send his men. But there was one person in Havana who was close to her at one time and it was possible that she would try to visit him. It was a hunch, but it was all he had for the time being. The revolt lost its energy many years ago and his network of informers had long decayed. It would take much time and money to re-establish it, so until then he had to depend on his wits. And his wits told him to keep a close eye on Tomas Enrique de Rosa.

- 11 -

Pauline woke to the smell of coffee. For a brief moment she thought she was home, but when she reached across the bed for Zeke she realized she was alone. She rubbed her eyes then sat up, the mattress on which she sat firm yet comfortable. The house where she resided was small and functional, common for most workers in the mountainous region. She sighed then lay back on the bed. She missed Zeke; she missed the farm; she missed Freedonia. This was the reason why she never let herself get close to anyone during the revolt. Love was a distraction, making one too cautious, too careful. But she would not be able to go home until she fulfilled her mission. The thought of it made her angry. She had not asked to be involved, no matter how important. If her old friends had sent for her to return for their sake she may have said yes. She would have immediately refused if she knew it involved a power game between warring nations. Her anger drove the final dregs of sleep from her mind.

Pauline dressed then entered Mama Corrine's kitchen. Coffee brewed in the pot hanging over the fireplace, while warm cups of milk sat on the table surrounding two wicker baskets filled with tostadas and fruit. Mama Corrine prepared three plates with eggs, bacon and potatoes. As she went about her work Dominic entered the house cradling a stack of wood.

"*Buenos dias,*" he said.

"*Buenos dias,*" she replied.

Mama Corrine turn then smiled.

"Ah, you are awake! Good, good!"

Pauline sat at the table and Mama Corrine served her a plate. She waited until Corrine and Dominic sat before sipping her coffee. She closed her eyes and smiled.

"I forgot how good coffee could be," she said.

"You forgot many things."

Corrine and Dominic shared glances. Pauline frowned.

"I didn't," she replied.

"So why didn't you come back?" Dominic asked.

"I don't know." "In the beginning we waited for word to return. Messages we sent were never answered."

"Intercepted most likely," Corrine said. "The Spaniards were ruthless. So many died."

"We should have stayed," Pauline said.

"You would be dead if you did," Dominic said. His face became hard. "It was Senor de Rosa's idea."

Pauline lowered her head. The worst thing about Dominic's words was that she knew he was right. De Rosa was her father by blood only.

Mama Corrine placed her hands on their shoulders.

"There is no need for anger," she said. "We cannot change the past. We can, however, change the future."

"By serving the whims of the Freedonians?" Pauline asked.

"It doesn't matter why they're here," Corrine said. "They will help us for their own reasons then they will leave. Cuba will be ours."

Pauline was skeptical. "Will they leave?"

"Yes," Dominic answered. "Freedonia has no interest in controlling Cuba. They have bigger concerns."

She took another sip of coffee.

" I don't care what their concerns are. I want to finish this for Cuba. If that means serving the interest of Freedonia so be it. I know the Freedonians are not power hungry like the Europeans or Americans. They have no ambitions for a great empire like the New Haitians. They wish only to exist in peace, but they are more than willing to defend themselves."

Corrine shook her head. "Isn't it ironic that the only way that we can have peace is to be prepared for war?"

"It is," Pauline said.

"Enough talk," Corrine said. "Your breakfast is getting cold and we have much to do."

They completed the meal in silence, Pauline's thoughts drifting back to Zeke. She knew he was looking for her, at least if he had any idea she was still alive. A pain emerged in her chest; what if he was told she was dead?"

"I have to send a message to Zeke," she said.

"No," Dominic replied. "Any attempt to contact anyone outside our group might reveal our position."

"I must," she said. "He needs to know that I'm alive."

"Your boyfriend will have to wait," Dominic said. "There are more important matters than sending love letters."

"You'll get nothing from me until I do so,' "Pauline said.

"Did you . . ."

Pauline kicked Dominic in the stomach. He staggered toward the door, his face in shock. He managed to block the punch aimed for his face but realized too late his error. Pauline kicked him again, this time in the chest. Dominic fell through the door.

"La Rosa! No!" Corrine shouted.

Pauline ignored her. She was tired of people telling her what to, tired of being manipulated.

Dominic was standing, a grin on his face.

"Not bad," he said. He swayed then fell into a smooth ginga.

Pauline grinned. So, Dominic was a capoerista. This would be interesting.

Pauline feinted and Dominic attempted to sweep her legs. She sprang back then dodged the hands sweeping for her face. Dominic's heel glanced her chin, sending her staggering back. As he cartwheeled toward her Pauline kicked his arms. Dominic collapsed onto his head. Pauline moved in. She grabbed Dominic into a choking grip, her legs locking his arms to his side. She squeezed just enough to warn him what she was capable of.

"A rose has thorns," she whispered. "You would do well to remember."

She choked him until he was near unconsciousness before releasing him. Pauline dusted her clothes as she stood. Corrine rushed to Dominic's side, but he waved her away. He remained on the ground, pulling his legs up to his chest then draping his arms over his knees. To Pauline's surprise he smiled.

"I wondered why they revered you so," he said, his voice strained.

"It has nothing to do with her fighting skills," Corrine said.

"You were a good teacher, Mama," Pauline said.

"And you were my best pupil," Corrine answered.

Dominic looked between them both before standing.

"I'll send the note personally. But we do have more pressing matters to discuss."

Pauline continued adjusting her clothes as she walked to the rocking chair on Mama Corinne's porch. Dominic rubbed his throat as he leaned on the roof support.

"Everyone is ready to act," he said.

"I know," Pauline replied. "But we have to make sure whatever we do will count. No more wasted lives. We leave the planters out of it this time."

"We need their support," Dominic replied. "We have to finance the revolution."

Pauline spat. "It's because of them the revolution died. They were so easy to take New Spain's crumbs and sell us out. They're dogs."

"You speak of your own father."

"My father by blood only," she said. Pauline was lying. He was more than that, but it didn't stop her from hating him.

"Sooner or later we'll need their help," Dominic said. "The Freedonians won't be here forever. We might as well ask for it now."

"And give them the chance to betray us before we act? No."

Pauline fell silent for a moment, and then began rocking.

"Are the sugar plantations still the major source of wealth for the island?

"Yes," Dominic said.

Pauline smiled. "Then we will strike them first. We'll take the workers with us to bolster our ranks and burned the fields."

"How many will we strike?" Dominic asked.

Pauline looked at him and grinned. "All of them."

Dominic's eyes went wide. "All of them? That's impossible!"

Mamma Corrine joined them on the porch.

"La Rosa has returned. Nothing is impossible."

"We need to draw the soldiers' attention to the interior while we search for this ship the Freedonians are afraid of. You'll contact Scobel and give him a list of everything we'll need. They'll pay us to do their dirty work."

"And what will you do while I'm busy with all this?" Dominic asked.

Pauline smiled. "Visit an old friend."

* * *

Alejandra Cabeza de Espinoza loved horse riding so much she rode every day. Her estate, which overlooked Havana and its scenic harbor, was a horse rider's dream, with numerous paths and a large number of fences for jumping. She and her husband Antonio amassed a fortune from inheritance and the merchant trade, indulging each other with extravagant gifts. Their wealth also paid for their detachment from politics. During the revolution they supported both sides which served as insurance for their businesses and their personal property. Antonio favored the interests of New Spain; Alejandra shared her money with the rebels. Alejandra also had a personal reason to aid the rebels, one she kept to herself.

Alejandra strode into her house after a particularly strenuous ride, her white blouse sweat stained about the armpits. At first glance one would think she was direct Spanish descent, but closer examination revealed her Yoruba blood. People called her mulatta, a term she accepted as gracefully as she did any other words anyone used to describe her. She thought herself above such labels.

Alejandra heard her maid Charo clear her throat. She turned to see the diminutive woman standing with a lovely dark-skinned woman bearing a bouquet of flowers. It took every bit of her control to keep from screaming out loud with joy.

"Yes, Charo?" she said.

"*Senora*, this woman brought these flowers for you," Charo said. "She claims she was instructed to deliver them to you personally."

"Leave us," Alejandra said.

Charo bowed then left the room. Alejandra looked to make sure the maid was gone before rushing the woman with the flowers and hugging her tight.

"Paulina!" she squealed. "I thought I'd never see you again!"

Pauline dropped the flowers and returned Alejandra's hug.

"It has been too long, *hermana*,' she replied. "Much too long."

Alejandra released Pauline then grabbed her hand, dragging her to the couch.

"Where did you go? Why did you leave? Are you well? You must tell me everything!"

Pauline laughed and hugged Alejandra again. They grew up as best friends, each the sibling the other did not have. Though their backgrounds were vastly different, Pauline and Alejandra attended the same schools because of Pauline's father's status. They were immediately drawn to each other, Pauline to Alejandra because of her easy-going ways unfettered by class and status, and Alejandra to Pauline for the same reasons. The end of their education saw them return to their social status; Pauline labored with her mother in the streets of Havana while Alejandra married Antonio, forging a wealthy union between families. But both women refused to let their different lives destroy their friendship. When Pauline decided to join the revolution Alejandra did as well, using her influence and position to support the cause.

Alejandra's joy drained from her face, replaced by a stern gaze.

"You left without telling me," she said. 'I was heartbroken. For ten years I have not heard from you. How could you do that to me, *hermana*?"

"Things happened so fast," Pauline said. "We had to leave as soon as possible. Maceo and Gomez were safe because of their status. I was expendable, so I had to go into hiding. I could tell no one, especially you."

"I didn't speak to Antonio for months!" Alejandra exclaimed. "Our marriage hasn't been the same since."

"I see you are still married to him," Pauline commented.

"He has certain talents I enjoy," Alejandra replied.

The two of them giggled like the girls they once were. They could never be angry with each other for long. Pauline cursed herself for cutting Alejandra from her life. At that moment she realized how much she missed her.

"It doesn't matter," Alejandra said. "You are here now. But I am curious as to why."

"The revolution has begun again," she answered.

"It never ended," Alejandra said. "Either that or someone has been taking my money for nothing."

Pauline hesitated for a moment, wondering if she should share all she knew. The look on her best friend's face said all she needed to know.

"It's different this time," she said. "The Freedonians are involved."

"They are no better than the Spaniards," Alejandra said.

"Not exactly," Pauline said. "It is because of them that I am here. They want something, but they are not interested in controlling Cuba. Still, we don't want to be completely dependent on them. Which is why I have come to you."

"What do you need?" Alejandra asked.

"We need guns and ammunition," Pauline replied.

"Done. Follow me."

Alejandra stood then led Pauline through her expansive house to her bedroom. The room was exquisite, white furniture arranged around a sumptuous rice bed with a laced canopy. Pauline followed Alejandra into a closet larger than most Cubans' homes. She shoved aside a row of dresses, revealing what appeared to be a bare wall. She tapped the wall three times and a panel swung open, revealing a combination safe. Alejandra opened the safe then took out a long tray. She opened the tray and extracted a sizable bag.

"It's gold," she said. "Take it. It should buy you enough weapons for a start. I'll send more later."

Pauline took the bag.

"Thank you, *hermana*. Thank you so much. I feel bad coming to see you after so long to ask you for money."

Alejandra dispelled Pauline's awkwardness with a wave of her hand.

"You are my *hermana*. I'll do anything for you, as you have done for me."

They left the bedroom, returning to the foyer.

"There is one more thing I must ask," Pauline said.

"What is it?"

Pauline hesitated again. "Can you . . . can you contact my father?"

Alejandra's expression softened.

"Of course, I can," she said.

"Tell him I'm coming to see him. I have no specific day or time, but I will come to see him soon."

"I will visit him personally," Alejandra said.

The women embraced again.

"When will I see you again?" Alejandra asked.

"I don't know, but you will see me again, *hermana*."

She kissed Alejandra's cheek.

"This I promise."

Pauline exited the house and hurried down the walkway to the main street. Her meeting with Alejandra was too short, but she had work to do. She prayed that she would be able to keep her promise.

- 1 2 -

Zeke entered Savannah resembling a vagabond. His face was soiled with sand from the road and dust billowed from his clothes as he jiggled down the uneven paver brick road that edged Savannah harbor. He rode straight to the docks, determined to be on the next ship to Cuba. But he didn't expect to arrive in such a state. He was exhausted and needed a bath and a bit of rest before continuing his pursuit of Pauline. Instinct told him to push on, but experience told him a dirty man smelling like a barn would stand out even among the most common crowd.

He guided the noisy motorbike to the first hotel he came upon. He shut off the engine then lifted the bike onto the sidewalk, leaning it against the hotel wall before staggering into the lobby. He waved off the curious concierge as he trudged to the check-in counter. The receptionist attempted to smile as Zeke's fragrance invaded her nose.

"Welcome to the Grand," she said with a wavering smile. "You seem a little worse for wear."

Zeke grinned. "That was a good try. I'm tired and I stink." He reached into his pocket, pulled out a handful of eagles and slammed them on the desk. "How fast can I get a room?"

"I'll see to it immediately, sir," the receptionist replied.

Zeke filled out the paperwork, paid for the night then took his room key from the lovely lady and headed to his room. To his relief the hotel had indoor plumbing so he didn't have to wait for someone to draw his bath. He stripped off his clothes, ran a tubful of steaming hot water then jumped in,

"Sweet Lord!" he exclaimed as the hot water loosened his knotted muscles and washed away his aches. He fell asleep immediately; when he woke, he soaked in a dingy tub of lukewarm water. He drained the tub, and then ran more water, this time scrubbing off the grime. He dressed in fresh clothing then headed to the harbor in search of the first ship bound for Cuba.

The harbormaster's office occupied a bleached tabby stone lighthouse standing on a manmade outcrop of granite. Zeke knocked before entering.

"Come on in," a gruff voice shouted.

The harbormaster was a chubby red-faced man with a warm smile. A fiddler's cap sat on his bulbous head, strands of straw blond hair extending beyond the rim. The bottle of open Scotch on his desk probably had much to do with his demeanor.

"Hey," Zeke said as he tipped his hat. "I'm Zeke Culpepper and I'm looking to be on the first boat heading to Havana, Cuba. What you got?"

The harbormaster's right eyebrow rose. "Cuba, eh? Let's find out."

The harbormaster took a swig of scotch then grabbed the thick ledger on his desk and dragged it before him. He flipped the book open, squinting as he ran his finger down the pages. After a few moments searching he shook his head.

"No passenger ships headed to Havana for at least two weeks," he said. "Got a few cargo ships and a whaler leaving tomorrow."

"That'll do," Zeke said. "Where do I find the captains?"

"Check out the Salty Dog," the harbormaster said. "The captains may not be there, but some of the crew surely will. They can direct you to the captains."

The harbormaster scribbled on a piece of paper then handed it to Zeke.

"Here's a list of the ships. Take a right out the door and keep walking. You can't miss it."

Zeke tilted his hat. "Much obliged."

"Good luck and be careful," the harbormaster warned. "Those sea dogs tend to get a bit rowdy before they set sail. A city boy like you might get roughed up a bit."

Zeke grinned. "Thanks for the information and the warning. I can take care of myself."

Zeke hurried down the cobblestone road to the modest brick building known as The Salty Dog. A sign decorated with the fading image of a dog draped in a yellow water slicker hung over the entrance. The battered door opened into a cramped watering hole filled with rough looking men and women drinking hard and cursing loud. Zeke didn't have time to sift through the crowd to inquire about the captains; he needed answers fast.

"Hey!" he shouted. "Listen up!"

The crowd gradually grew quiet, hostile eyes focusing on Zeke. He ignored the glares as he unfolded the list given to him by the harbormaster.

"I'm looking for the captains of the *Zephyr*, *Fool's Errand*, or the *Motley Crew*," he said. "Any of you working these ships?"

A large man with blond hair and piercing blue eyes stood.

"What's it to you?" he said.

"I'm looking for passage to Cuba," Zeke replied.

"These ain't no passenger ships," the man said. "These are working boats. We ain't got no room for freeloaders."

Zeke knew where this was headed. He placed his hands on his hips.

"I think that's the captain's decision, not yours."

"Well, today I'm speaking for the captains and I say get the hell out of here while you can still walk."

Zeke looked about the room. "Can anyone else direct me to the captains?"

The big blond brute shoved his way through the throng then lunged at Zeke. Zeke side-stepped the attack, then drove his foot between the man's legs. The man crumpled to the floor, curling around his damaged gonads. A skinny brown-skinned man jumped up from one of the small tables, yelled and then charged Zeke. The man threw a wide haymaker at Zeke's head; Zeke blocked the punch and hit the man across the jaw with a stinging right cross that sent him to the floor atop the other man.

Zeke rubbed his knuckles as he knelt over the pile.

"That was a cheap shot," he said to the big man. "But I'm in a hurry."

His eyes focused on the unconscious skinny man.

"As for you, you were just stupid."

"I'll take you to them."

A woman emerged from the crowd, umber skinned and stocky. Her headwrap towered above her, making her seem taller. She wore a loose jeans and a canvas shirt; her bracelets jangled as she extended her hand to Zeke. Zeke took it and entered into a firm handshake.

"Name's Zenobia," she said. "Who might you be?"

"Zeke Culpepper."

"Glad to meet you," she said. "Anybody who can put a whooping on those two scalawags is alright by me. Come on, I'll take you to the *Zephyr*'s captain."

"Thank you, ma'am," Zeke said.

"You can drop the ma'am. Just call me Zenobia. I ain't been a ma'am for a while."

Zenobia grinned, flashing her gold tooth. Zeke tipped his hat then followed the woman from The Salty Dog and back out into the streets. They left the harbor district and entered into Savannah proper with its neatly arranged streets and beautiful homes.

"Where we going?" Zeke asked.

"Lulabelle's," Zenobia answered. "It's an establishment for those with means. They serve food, drink and whatever else their clientele desires."

"That's kind of high living for a sea captain," Zeke commented.

"One captain owns all three ships you mentioned," Zenobia answered. "She's a wealthy woman indeed. I don't know why she still sails out with them. I guess she loves the work, although I don't understand why anyone would."

"I take it you ain't partial to this line of work."

"No sir!" Zenobia answered. "My family worked the boats for generations, shrimpers mostly. Daddy hit on hard times a few years ago and had to sell the boat. Been laboring for other folks since then. I never liked it and I still don't. I'm saving my money to take a blimp to Atlanta. I heard they're so many jobs people can ask what they want for pay."

"Don't believe everything you hear," Zeke warned.

"You ever been to Atlanta?" Zenobia asked.

"That's where I'm from," Zeke replied. "If you're a hard worker and got your mind set right it's a great place to be. Otherwise you're just going to be a different kind of poor."

They strolled up to a large structure surrounded by a verdant garden embracing a majestic fountain. The edifice resembled the large plantation homes that one existed throughout Freedonia, remnants of a time long ago when most of the people in the land were enslaved. Thick columns rose on either side of the elaborate entrance, with two well-dressed doormen flanking the beautifully carved door.

"The captain is inside," Zenobia said. "Just asked for Catherine Bedford."

"You ain't coming?" Zeke asked.

"They don't allow my kind in there," Zenobia replied.

Zeke frowned. "They will today. Come on."

Zeke and Zenobia climbed the steps to the wide porch. One doorman greeted Zeke with a wide smile and a handshake; the other met Zenobia with a sneer and a stare.

"Welcome to Lulabelle's," the doorman said. "What brings you to our establishment this fine day?"

"I'm looking for Catherine Bedford," he said. "Zenobia here tells me she's inside."

"You can't take her word," the other doorman said. They'll say anything for an eagle."

"Watch your manners," Zeke warned. "The lady is with me."

The doormen looked at each other in confusion. The man on the right, obviously the senior doorman began to speak.

"Sir, I don't think . . ."

Zeke grabbed Zenobia's hand then pushed his way between the befuddled doormen. He opened the door to a grand scene; well-heeled men and women sat around circular tables as attractive waiters swirled among them like dancers. The sight of such a sumptuous feast reminded Zeke he hadn't had breakfast. He was suddenly famished.

"Welcome to Lulabelle's!" a female voice sang.

Zeke turned to see the greeter. She was as lovely as the waiters, her brown eyes kind and attentive. Those same eyes shifted then focused over his shoulder as she raised her gloved hand. Zeke turned to see the doormen backing out, their facial expressions apologetic.

"I apologize for the inconvenience," the woman said. "How can I help you?"

Zeke tipped his hat. "Hey. I'm Zeke Culpepper and this is Zenobia . . ."

"Wright," Zenobia finished.

Zeke almost laughed when he looked at Zenobia. She resembled a sheep that had stumbled into a den of wolves.

He turned his attention back to the greeter.

"Are you Lulabelle?" he asked.

The woman's laugh was like church bells ringing.

"Of course not! Miss Lulabelle is entertaining clients. I'm the manager, Christine Ambrosia. Are you here for lunch?"

"I don't know," Zeke replied. "I hear this is a place for exclusive clientele."

"I can look at your demeanor and tell you fit the bill," Christine said.

"What about my companion?" Zeke asked. "Your doormen didn't seem to be that happy with her."

"Our doormen can be quite rude sometimes," Christine said.

"There she is!" Zenobia pointed to a table near the center of the restaurant. An elegant middle-aged woman sat alone, delicately slicing the large rib eye steak on her plate.

"Ah, Miss Bedford," Christine said. "She always takes lunch alone. I assume you are in shipping?"

"Something like that," Zeke said. "We'll take a table if you don't mind."

"Excellent!" Christine sang.

"And can you share a message with Miss Bedford?"

Christine smiled. "I can try."

Zeke slipped her two gold eagles. "Let her know me and Miss Wright are here to see her. This should help your efforts."

"It certainly will," Christine replied. "This way, please."

Zeke and Zenobia followed Christine to a table near Miss Bedford. Curious yet respectful eyes followed them, a few patrons nodding to Zeke as he sat.

"You're causing quite a stir," Christine said.

Zeke almost answered but kept quiet. Under other circumstances he would enjoy having an interesting conversation with Christine, but he knew where his heart was.

"Here are your menus," Christine said. "Darrell will be your waiter. He will be with you shortly. Enjoy!"

Zeke watched Christine glide to Miss Bedford's table then whisper in her ear. She strolled away; soon afterwards Miss Bedford tilted her head and glanced in their direction.

"Hello Mr. Culpepper!"

Zeke jumped. He twisted about to see a waiter standing next to him.

"Damn man! You like to scared the . . .sense out of me."

Darrell laughed. He was a tall, skinny ebony man with a big grin.

"I beg your pardon," he said, his voice deep like an old river. "Welcome to Lulabelle's. I'll be your waiter for the afternoon. What would you like to drink?"

"Tea," Zeke said.

"And for the lady?"

"A mint julep," Zenobia replied.

Zeke grinned and Zenobia shrugged her shoulders.

"I may be looking for work tomorrow because of you," she explained. "I might as well get something out of it."

"That's true," Zeke agreed. "Order whatever you like."

Zenobia's eyes widened. "Really?"

"Really," Zeke replied. "I owe you."

Darrell returned with their drinks then took their orders. Zeke kept his eyes on Miss Bedford as her waiter cleared her table. She paid the waiter, stood and straightened her dress, then came directly to their table, her curious eyes focused on him. Zeke stood then took her extended hand, kissing it.

"Catherine Bedford," she said.

"I know," Zeke replied. "I'm . . ."

"Zeke Culpepper," Catherine finished. "I see Zenobia led you to me."

"I'm so sorry, Captain," Zenobia said. "I hope you're not upset."

"Not at all," Miss Bedford replied. "It seems Mr. Culpepper is seeking passage on one of my vessels and I'm always intrigued by an interested party with means."

Darrell brought Catherine a chair and she sat.

"So, tell me, Mr. Culpepper, what is it that you do?"

"I'm a collector," Zeke said.

Catherine leaned closer to him. "Really? And what do you collect, Mr. Culpepper?"

"Bounties," Zeke replied.

Catherine tossed her head back as she laughed.

"So you're a bounty hunter. By your garments I'll guess you're very successful."

Zeke grinned. "I have my good days and bad days."

"You don't say?" Catherine gave him a smile that revealed her curiosity went beyond business.

"Let's get to the point," Zeke said. "I need to get to Cuba as soon as possible and I hear you have a ship leaving tonight. I'd like to be on that ship and I'm willing to pay a pretty eagle to make it happen."

"You have been quite generous with your money," Catherine said. "But it's not just the gold eagles. A man seeking to leave with such haste is either chasing something or running away. Which means it's a very good possibility he is doing something illegal."

"I'm following someone," he said.

"A bounty?"

"No."

"This is intriguing."

"Look, Miss Bedford . . ."

"Catherine, please."

Zeke sighed. "Look, Catherine, I hate to be rude but if you don't want my business then let me know so I can get on about finding someone who does."

"Calm down, Mr. Culpepper," Catherine said. "I'm interested. A person has to ask questions. As a ship owner I'm always approached with business propositions and many of them are illicit."

"I can assure you that everything I do is aboveboard," Zeke said.

Catherine stood. "In that case, I welcome your business. Meet me at the docks this evening about 8:00 P.M. The *Zephyr* sets sail then."

"Thank you, ma'am," Zeke said. "Much obliged."

"Don't be late," she said, then strolled away.

"That was close," Zenobia said.

"I'll deal with you later, Zenobia," Catherine called out as she exited Lulabelle's.

"I'll be damned!" Zenobia cried. The arrival of her meal calmed her.

"Eat up," Zeke said. "It's on me."

Zeke ate his fill as well. He had no idea what kind of food to expect once he arrived in Cuba, but he knew what waited for him on a ship. This would be his last good meal for a while.

- 1 3 -

Pauline spied on her father from the shadows, a tempest of emotions roiling her stomach and making her nauseous. Tomas Enrique de Rosa sat on his veranda under the porch fan, a glass of spiced rum in his right hand, a cigar in his left. He looked out on the dark harbor, a content expression on his copper hued middle-aged face. Pauline remembered many nights watching him from hiding as she did now, knowing that if she was caught it would cause trouble for her and her mother. She would sneak out of the house and follow him to the plantation after his visits. Then she would marvel at the beautiful home and life which he lived separate from them. In the beginning she longed to be a part of it, but as she grew older that longing turned to bitterness. Growing sugar was arduous work, even for a man who did as little of it as Tomas. His days as a planter were over; Tomas had become a distributor of the same product he had once created with the hands of others. The profits were higher and the dangers much less.

"You are still smoking those terrible cigars," she said.

Tomas stiffened. He turned toward her, peering into the dark with a knowing expression.

Alejandra had visited him two days ago and told him she was coming.

Pauline emerged from shadows. Tomas placed his rum on the small table nearby and put out his cigar in his ashtray. He stood then extended his arms in expectation.

"Paulina," he said.

Pauline stopped just short of his embrace, folding her arms across her chest.

"Popi," she replied.

His smile faded as he lowered his arms.

"It is wonderful to see you," he said. "It's been so long."

"Ten years," Pauline said.

Tomas returned to his chair.

"How was your time in Freedonia?" he asked. Pauline's eyes went wide and he grinned.

"You knew I was there?"

Tomas nodded as he sipped his rum. "Of course. I made the arrangements and paid the expenses."

"You?"

Tomas frowned. "Despite what you think of me, I am your popi and I care about you. I love you. Nothing can change that."

Pauline opened her mouth as if to retort but didn't. She closed her eyes, marshalling her emotions. When she re-opened them, her demeanor was more professional.

"I don't need your love," she said. "I need your help."

"Are you back with the rebels?" he asked.

"Of course."

"Then I can be of no help to you, unless you plan on giving up that foolishness and returning to Freedonia."

He was bringing the cigar to his lips when Pauline stomped up to him then slapped it out of his hand. She crushed it under her shoe.

"Ten years ago, the planters were with us," she said. "Today they prosper and the workers still suffer."

"We made a deal with the devil," Tomas explained. "We agreed to lay down our arms and in exchange New Spain would pardon those involved and give us greater autonomy. But your friends refused. You refused."

Tomas opened his cigar box and took out another cigar. His cool demeanor had always annoyed her and continued to do so. It was if her life was just another thing for him to own and control. Life had been harsh for her and her mother because of his neglect. Her mother, Maria, was young, beautiful and naïve; Tomas was handsome and rich. Their affair had been brief yet long enough to scar them both. His wife, Elena, threatened to have their marriage annulled if he did not end the affair and disown her and her mother. Raul, her stepfather, discovered the affair and left her and mama to fend for themselves. Tomas helped when he could, but it was never enough. Mama came to hate him, as did Pauline.

"Why did you come back?" he asked.

"I had no choice," Pauline answered. "The Freedonians informed the government of my whereabouts. They have an interest here but don't want to get their hands dirty."

Tomas lowered his cigar. "Do they now? That changes everything. My friends would not act to support the workers, but they would be very interested knowing the Freedonians are involved."

"You can't tell them," Pauline replied.

"Then I cannot help you, Paulina. Not this time."

"At least use your contacts to help us find what the Freedonians are looking for."

"You mean this?"

Tomas reached into his pocket then extracted a folded piece of paper. He pushed it across the table; Pauline picked it up then unfolded it. She smiled.

"I think this is what you are looking for."

"Yes. Gracias popi. I will..."

Tomas looked over Pauline's shoulders then nodded. She turned to see a pair of lights moving toward his house. The lights halted then shut off.

"Were you followed?" Tomas asked.

"What?"

"Were you followed?" he asked again.

"Not that I know of."

It was probably General Gomez's men, Pauline thought. She took out her revolver then pointed it at her father. His eyes widened.

"Have you lost your senses?"

"No. I'm trying to save your life. Put down that damn cigar, raise your hands and stand up," she said.

"What's going on?" he asked.

"Either there is a traitor among us or Gomez figured out I would come see you," she said. "We must make this visit lookdifficult."

Pauline raised the gun to his face.

"You do that too easily," he said.

"Don't think I haven't thought about it," Paulina replied. "I'm going to hit you with my gun."

Tomas's eyes widened. "I don't think that's necessary."

"This has to look authentic,' she replied.

"I understand," Tomas said. He swallowed then braced himself. "I'll talk to my friends. I will send you their reply whatever they decide."

"Thank you, father," Pauline said.

She flipped the gun then struck him hard. Tomas collapsed to the floor.Pauline checked her father's pulse. He was still alive. She strolled to the back of the house as if she wasn't aware of the approaching interlopers, and then took off at a full sprint down the narrow street behind her father's house. She almost reached the end of the road when she stopped then crouched low. She heard voices; whoever figured she would visit her father probably was aware of how she would arrive unseen. She inched down the road, listening as she came closer to the street corner.

"You need to hire better men," she whispered as she holstered her revolver then took out her machete.

Pauline trotted to the end of the building then shoulder rolled into the open. She drove her fist between the first guards' legs then sidestepped as he fell to the ground whimpering. Her machete flew from her hand, its blade piercing the soldier across the street in the stomach. She sprinted to him, snatching the blade from his gut as she disappeared down the next street. Gunfire caused her to freeze, expecting the feeling of hot lead to bloom in her back. When it didn't, she turned to see the first man shooting his gun in the air, apparently signaling for the others. The fact that he wasn't shooting at her meant they were to take her alive. Pauline hurried down street after street, following an old escape route meant to confuse her pursuers and give her rescuers time to locate her. But there would be no rescue. She had insisted on coming alone, which at that moment she realized may have been a mistake. Pauline was hurrying down another narrow street when a door opened before her. A small woman stepped through the door; Pauline raised her machete instinctively, startling the woman. The woman raised her hands in surrender.

"I'm here to help you," she said. "Come inside quickly!"

Pauline had no choice. She rushed inside. The woman closed the door behind her. She smiled as she gestured toward the small table in the modest home.

"I have coffee," she said. "Would you like some?"

Pauline glanced toward the door, half expecting it to burst open at any moment. She looked back at the diminutive woman; her brown face creased with a genuine smile. She walked to the table then sat.

"Yes, I would," she finally said.

The woman shuffled to her stove, taking the blackened coffee pot then filling it with water. Her calm demeanor soothed Pauline despite her situation.

"My name is Juanita Perez," the woman said.

"*Hola*, Juanita," Pauline replied. "I'm . . ."

"I know who you are."

Pauline tensed. Her hand went to her machete. The woman peeked over her hunched shoulder then grinned.

"You have nothing to fear from me, *La Rosa*," the woman said. "When I was a girl, I would sit on the roof of this building when the nights were too hot to sleep inside. That was the first time I saw you. There was something different about you. I think it was the way you walked. So confident. So powerful."

Juanita shuffled back to the stove and began brewing the coffee.

"It was later when I discovered who you really were. I wanted to join the revolution, but I was too young."

Pauline let go of her machete then slumped in her chair.

"You were smart not to," Pauline replied. "The life of a rebel is not an easy one."

Juanita laughed. "I joined in my own way. Mama and I would give what we could to the people raising money to support the cause. We would sometimes share what we bought at the market."

"Thank you," Pauline said.

Juanita's face became solemn. "It was a terrible day when you left. At first it was rumored you were dead. I remember that day. I cried until I was sick. But then we learned that you escaped. No one knew where you were but everyone knew you were safe."

Juanita poured the coffee into the small cups then added a generous amount of sugar. She carried the cups to the table, placing one before Pauline. Pauline waited until her host was seated before sipping the hot brew.

"This is excellent," Pauline said.

"If there is one thing I know how to do, it's make a good cup of coffee," Juanita replied.

Their moment was interrupted by harsh voices outside Juanita's door.

"Are you sure?"
"Yes."
"Break it down, then."

Juanita and Pauline jumped to their feet. Pauline snatched out her revolver and machete. Juanita shook her head as she grabbed Pauline's coffee then dumped it in her sink. She guided Pauline to her bedroom. Juanita grunted as she pushed the bed aside to reveal a stairwell.

"It leads to the city sewers," Juanita said. "Like I said, we supported the revolution. It won't be pleasant, of course, but you'll be safe."

Someone banged on the door.

"Open this door immediately!"

"Follow the main tunnel," Juanita said. "It will lead you to the harbor."

"Thank you," Pauline said.

"Thank you for returning," Juanita replied. "I have hope in my heart again. Now go. I'll handle the *fiana*."

Juanita handed Pauline a kerosene lantern. Pauline descended to the sewer as Juanita pushed the bed back in place. Guilt filled her heart as her feet sank into the muck. Everyone expected so much of her. She'd been betrayed to fulfill a mission for the Freedonians and that was her intention. But so many others expected so much more from her. As she trudged through the dark tunnel, she decided that she would not leave after her mission. She would stay for her people. She would stay for the revolution.

- 14 -

Zeke couldn't rest. After making arrangements with Miss Bedford, the anxiousness returned in full force. Every moment without Pauline increased the possibility she might be lost to him forever. Another thought grew in his mind as well, one that began to undermine his concern. Pauline had hidden an entire life from him. What other secrets would be revealed once they were reunited? Did he really know this woman he had fallen in love with?

Love. Yes, that's what it was. He couldn't deny it any longer. He'd been in love one other time and what he felt for Pauline was way beyond that former relationship. It was the reason he was working every favor and bringing more attention to himself than he preferred. It was another reason to find her, so she could explain herself and he could determine if his love was built on a foundation of lies.

There was no use trying to rest. Zeke abandoned his room then took to the streets of Savannah. He strolled down the avenues, admiring the old architecture and musing on the enslaved hands that built it. Those days were long gone, but there were still those who would jump at the chance to bring them back again. He fought against them during the Reunion War not as a Freedonian, but with

New Haiti when the fickle nation finally decided to enter the conflict on Freedonia's side. The war ended quickly after that, but not fast enough for Zeke. The fighting between the Haitians and the Americans took brutality to another level, which was probably why the hostilities ended so quickly. The Americans showed no mercy, and neither did the Haitians. The harsh terms of American capitulation left deep wounds that had yet to heal.

Zeke took supper at a small kitchen near the edge of the city, the type of place where hardworking locals ended their day. He enjoyed a hearty bowl of gumbo with cornbread and tea, a meal that soothed his stomach but not his anxiety. With the sun setting he hurried back to his hotel, packed his things. Zeke paid his bill, then headed to the docks.

Zeke spotted the man and woman as soon as he stepped out of the hotel. They pretended to be engaged in small talk, but Zeke had pulled the ruse too many times himself to be fooled by it. He ambled down the street a few blocks then hailed a carriage. The buggy chugged to the curb then stopped, the steam cloud from the exhaust washing over Zeke and the driver.

"Where to, sir?" the driver asked.

"The harbor," Zeke said. "And take the scenic route."

"That's going to cost you an extra eagle," the driver said.

"I'm good for it," Zeke replied.

He climbed into the wagon and it rambled away. Zeke took a peek behind him and spied the man and woman hailing their own transportation. The vehicle they summoned was not a public taxi. He leaned closer to the driver.

"Another eagle if you can show me what this thing can do," he whispered.

The driver took a glance behind them.

"You must be in some kind of trouble," the driver said.

"Maybe," Zeke replied.

"Two more eagles and I'll lose them for sure," the driver said. He reached back toward Zeke with an open hand. Zeke pressed two eagles into his palm.

"Let's do it."

The man stuffed the coins into his pocket then reached for a lever beside his right foot.

"Sit back and hold on!" he warned.

The driver gripped the lever then shoved it forward. The engine roared and a cloud of steam exploded from the carriage's exhaust pipe. The carriage lurched forward, the force shoving Zeke back into his seat as the carriage surged down the street. Zeke looked back to see the man and woman pointing in their direction and waving their arms frantically. He tumbled into the side of the carriage as the driver veered right down another broad street. Zeke finally took the driver's advice and held on.

The driver made so many wild turns Zeke had no idea which direction they travelled. Rows of houses and live oaks finally gave way to the open harbor, docked ships bobbing on the brackish water. The driver pulled up to the tabby stone curb and the carriage skidded to a stop. He faced Zeke with a smirk on his face.

"Here you go," he said.

Zeke jumped out of the carriage then grabbed his bags.

"Much obliged."

The driver tipped his hat then sped away. Zeke checked his watch; he was ten minutes early. He took a minute to get his bearing then hurried to the rendezvous point. As he neared the dock, he saw Miss Bedford waiting. A man accompanied her, most likely a bodyguard. Zeke was almost upon them when he realized he was wrong. The man was definitely Freedonia Dispatch.

The man lifted his head, tipped his hat then grinned.

"Mr. Culpepper," he said. "It's good to see you. I'm . . ."

Zeke rushed up to the man then punched him in the face. He crumpled to the pavement unconscious. Miss Bedford's gloved hand covered her mouth as she gasped.

"You ratted me out!" Zeke said.

"I did no such thing!" Catherine replied. "He said he was a friend of yours."

"And you believed him?"

"Why shouldn't I? Mr. Culpepper, what type of calamity have you brought my way?"

Zeke was about to answer when he saw the carriage carrying the man and woman pull up in the distance. There was another car with it carrying two more men and women.

"Where's your ship?" he asked Catherine.

"At the end of the dock . . . Mr. Culpepper, if you think I'm going to honor this deal you have another thing coming!"

"Okay, then give me my money back," Zeke said

Catherine's face turned dour. "Well, I . . ."

"I thought so," Zeke said. "Now get along to your boat before these other folks see you. I'll be back directly."

Catherine nodded. "Don't you bring your troubles to my ship."

Zeke tipped his hat. "Don't worry. I won't."

Catherine trotted down the dock as Zeke walked toward the group. He was sure the man and woman belonged to Tubman; the others were most likely hired help. If they planned to kill him, they wouldn't need that much support. He was about to make their job a lot easier.

The group halted as he came closer, the man and the woman looking confused. The man's plain mocha face contrasted with the woman's ebony comeliness as their expressions shifted from bewilderment to stern. Zeke extended his arms in surrender.

"I guess you got me," he said. "Although I don't know why you're trying so hard."

"Don't play dumb, Ezekiel," the woman replied, her deep voice filled with authority. "You're attempting to interfere with a vital operation."

The man took a pair of handcuffs from his jacket, briefly exposing a .45 Banneker tucked under his arm and an ivory cross pinned to his collar. Yep, definitely Tubman's, Zeke mused.

Zeke waited until the cuffs were almost on his wrist before he lunged, kicking the man in the balls then smashing an uppercut into his face as he bent forward in pain. He kicked the woman in the stomach before she could move. She fell to the dock, clutching her gut. Zeke sidestepped the first ruffian's attack and tripped him; his hands went up blocking the left jab/right cross combination of the second man. He was about to throw a combination of his own when someone grasped him around the waist from behind, lifted him off his feet then slammed him to the ground. He grimaced as he landed on his left arm. Zeke rolled away from the woman trying to stomp him with her sharpened heels. He rose to a crouch then spun, knocking the bulky woman off her feet. The other two were going for their guns.

"The hell with orders," one of them said. "I'm killing this sumabitch!"

Zeke whipped his lever action shotgun from under his jacket the fired twice, blowing both men onto their backs, their chests filled with buckshot.

He tucked the gun back into his jacket, and then sprinted to the end of the dock.

"I sure hope they weren't Tubman's folks," he said. "If they were this, will be a one way . . ."

Something caught his ankle and he fell. He threw out his hands, saving his face by falling on his palms. He kicked back instinctively and was answered by a low grunt. Zeke scrambled to his feet as the man he knocked out earlier stood as well. The two battled toe to toe, their speed and skill resembling that of the prizefights that took place in the Peachtree Stadium in Atlanta. The man was good; too good in fact. If Zeke didn't take him out soon, he'd miss his ship and fall into the agents' hands. He lowered his guard enough to make his opponent think there was an opening. Zeke ducked the right cross meant for his jaw then dipped his shoulder as the man fell over. Zeke crouched, catching man on his upper back then wrapping his arms around his torso. Once he knew he had him he carried him to the edge of the dock then threw him into the harbor.

Zeke didn't wait to hear the splash; he ran down the dock to Catherine's ship. Two crew members were lifting the gangplank when he arrived.

"Wait!" he shouted. "I'm a passenger!"

The men kept lifting the plank, ignoring Zeke.

"You heard the man! Put the damn gangplank down!" a familiar voice ordered.

The men dropped the gangplank and Zeke hurried aboard. He was greeted by Zenobia's smiling face.

"Hey Mr. Culpepper! We thought you changed you mind, or got caught."

"Neither of the two," Zeke replied. "But I am a bit worse for wear."

Zenobia looked him up and down. "Yeah, you could use a little attention. I saw you. You handle yourself pretty well."

Zeke eyes widened. "You saw me and you didn't help?"

"Not my fight," Zenobia said. "Besides, I just met you today. Come on below deck. I'll fix you up."

Zeke glanced back as he followed Zenobia. He was finally on his way. To what, he didn't know.

- 1 5 -

Gonzalez and his men stood over Tomas as he regained consciousness. The general frowned as he watched the man pull himself up then lean against the veranda.

"That's not the way a daughter should treat her father," he said.

Tomas looked contemptuously into the general's eyes. "If you knew me better, you'd know I probably deserved it."

Gonzales extended his hand but Tomas shook his head, refusing the gesture.

"I'll be fine," he said. "Shouldn't you be pursuing her instead of helping me?"

"That is being taken care of," Gonzales said.

"Who are you?" Tomas asked.

"Oh, I forget my manners. I am Comandante Philippe Gonzales. I'm the man in charge of bringing your daughter to justice and I think you can help us."

Tomas laughed. "Did you see what just happened?"

Philippe grinned. "Yes I did, and I consider it the best acting I've seen since my last visit to the Parisian theater."

Tomas tensed as his eyes narrowed.

"What are you implying, *Comandante*?"

Gonzales's smiled faded.

"Pick him up," he said.

The two men surged by Gonzales, grabbed Tomas's arms then lifted him to his feet.

"What are you doing!" he shouted. "What is the meaning of this?"

Gonzales walked by the men then opened the door to the house.

"Bring him," he said. He held the door open for his men as they dragged Tomas inside then he entered the house. Once inside Gonzales shut the door as the men tossed Tomas to the floor.

"Are you out of your mind?" Tomas said. "Do you know who I . . ."

Gonzales punched Tomas in the face. Tomas fell onto his back, his head striking the floor. He attempted to stand but Gonzales kicked him in the stomach. Tomas grimaced and closed his eyes as he fell again. When he opened them, the commander was standing over him.

"I know exactly who you are," Gonzales said. "You are a traitor to Cuba. You are a traitor to New Spain. You think your money and your position will protect you from the rule of law. But I am not one of your wealthy *hermanos*. I don't care who you know. My duty is to protect Cuba."

Philippe raised his foot. Tomas shifted, sweeping his other leg. The commander fell onto his back as Tomas stood. The other men came toward Tomas.

"No!" Philippe said. He stood then dusted off his clothes.

"So, you have some skill," he said. "Paulina had to learn from someone."

"I can claim no responsibility of who she came to be," Tomas said. "If I had been a better man, I could have. I don't know what you have come here for, *Comandante*, but if you expect me to beg for your mercy you've come to the wrong hacienda."

The commander attacked Tomas with a flurry of punches and kicks which Tomas easily deflected. The two men broke away from each other and circled, Tomas with an arrogant smile on his face that angered Gonzales. He knew that look well. He'd suffered from it many times as a boy and as a man.

"You have some skill," Tomas said. "But you fight like the trash you are. You grew up in the streets of Havana, scratching for a living until finding purpose and refuge in the military. I'm impressed that you reached the rank of comandante. Your kind usually rises no higher than sergeant. I'll have to say something about that to the Governor."

Tomas went on the offensive, landing two quick blows to Philippe's head followed by a kick to his gut. Gonzales doubled over but Tomas straightened him with a knee blow that sent him reeling backwards. Philippe caught himself on a chair then glared at Tomas.

"Kill him," he said.

The other men attacked. Tomas fought back as best he could, but they were too skilled. The blows slowly took their toll; Tomas fell to his knees after a blow to the jaw then was kicked onto his side. Blood filled his mouth as he rolled onto his back.

"Stop," Gonzales ordered. He took his revolver from his holster then marched over to the battered man.

"You won't get away with this," Tomas said.

"Yes, I will," Gonzales replied. "I fight for Cuba."

Tomas laughed and blood trickled from his mouth.

"Paulina will come for you."

Gonzales smiled. "Yes, she will."

He pressed the revolver barrel against Tomas's forehead, cocked the hammer, and then pulled the trigger.

- 16 -

The rumors were true; *La Rosa* had returned. Workers regained the hope that most thought would never return, defying the plantation owners' harsh demands and slave-like conditions. Children sang songs that were buried long ago, songs of freedom and equality. The authorities retaliated, dispersing any gatherings among the common folks with violence and heavily monitoring any celebrations with outward and covert force. And they scoured the island, hoping to find the woman who once again sparked the hopes of the downtrodden.

The cave was well-lit, its innards resembling that of a fortress. The damp walls bristled with racks of weapons and stacks of ammunition piled on the uneven floors. A large table occupied the cave's center, surrounded by men and women studying a large map of the island. Pauline leaned over the table, a narrow stick in her hand. Dominic stood beside her, his eyes shifting between the map and Pauline's intense face.

"The people are with us," she said. "Now we must show the governor we are serious. We strike the prisons."

Dominic leaned away, a frown on his face.

"The prisons? Why?"

"To fill our ranks," Pauline answered. "How many fighters do we have?"

"Eight hundred," Dominic replied. "Eight hundred trained and dedicated fighters. The last thing we need are criminals."

"Many of the inmates in these prisons are innocent," Pauline replied. "Freeing them will prove our commitment to the people. It will also be a blow to the governor's labor force."

Most of those at the table nodded in agreement. Though slavery had been abolished on the island a different type of servitude had been installed; prison labor. And it was very easy to become a prisoner, especially if one was poor. Constables arrested men and women for minor infractions and magistrates sentenced them to years of harsh labor, some sentences lasting as long as ten years. Most of those in the cave had been victims of the nefarious practice, which was why they did not protest Pauline's decision.

"We will strike *La Hacienda* first," Pauline decided.

A ripple of approval passed through the fighters. La Hacienda was Cuba's most notorious prison and the center of the forced labor system.

"I'm not sure of this plan," Dominic said.

"I am," Pauline replied.

She passed her gaze over everyone at the table. "Is there anyone else that does not think this is a good plan?

The other leaders shook their head. Pauline cut a mean glance at Dominic.

"Gather your fighters. We'll meet at the Ancestor Tree in three days."

The rebels filed out of the room. Dominic was about to join them when Pauline grabbed his arm.

"Dominic, a word," she said.

Dominic faced her, folding his arms across his chest.

"What is it, La Rosa?"

Pauline grinned. She'd only known the man a few weeks, but his ways were obvious. He was upset.

"You have to stop questioning my decisions," she said. "It's not good for the fighters to see us at odds. Any issues you have with my orders we settle in private. Understand?"

"This was not why you were brought here!" Dominic said. "We have a mission that we haven't even begun, and you want to lead a revolution!"

"I don't answer to the Freedonians," Pauline replied. "I did not ask to be here. But since I am, I'll finish what I started ten years ago. Besides, the mission has already begun."

"What are you talking about?"

Pauline reached into her pocket then took out a folded piece of paper. She handed it to Dominic.

"The location of New Spain's secret ship," she said.

Dominic unfolded the paper, and then studied it. Pauline grinned as his eyes widened.

"How did you get this? The Freedonians have been trying to locate this harbor for years."

"The Freedonians don't know my father," Pauline said. "Despite being a former rebel supporter, he has worked his way back into the graces of the government.

Dominic looked skeptical. "My information says you and your father do not get along."

Pauline frowned. "My father loves me. If there is a problem with our relationship, it's my problem, not his. He's always trying to make up for his mistakes. This information is another gesture."

Pauline pulled up a chair then sat at the table.

"What about the harbor?" Dominic asked.

"I have someone that will confirm my father's information," Pauline replied. "Once we are sure the ship is there, we will devise a plan."

"The attacks we launch over the next week serve everyone," she continued. "We'll free the prisoners and disrupt the sugar trade, which weakens the government's revenue stream and increases our support. It will also draw the government's attention to the interior. That will make it easier for us to reach the harbor and carry out the Freedonians' mission. That is if they supply us with the equipment we require."

Dominic folded the paper then handed it back to her.

"I'm impressed."

"Which is why you'll never question my decisions again. Understood?"

Dominic nodded. "Understood."

Pauline stood. "Now let's go. We have a country to liberate."

Dominic did not move. He stood still, staring at her as a smile grew on his face. The long look made her uncomfortable yet curious.

"Is there something else?" she asked.

"Not yet," he replied. "Maybe later, when things have settled."

Warmth came to her cheeks and she smiled before she knew it. It had been a long time since a man other than Zeke expressed interest in her. But this was not the time and Dominic was not the man. It was best she made things clear now so to avoid any awkward situations later.

"Dominic, let me explain something to you. I . . ."

"*La Rosa! La Rosa*!"

Pauline looked toward the cave entrance. Ermano, one of her most trusted men, ran to them, a rolled sheet of paper in his hand and a distraught look on his face.

"What is it?" she asked.

Ermano handed the paper to her.

"I'm sorry," he said.

Pauline unrolled the paper. It was a wanted poster for her arrest, the image of her taken ten years ago. It was the words that struck her hard.

'Paulina de Rosa, wanted for instigating rebellion against the sovereign state of Cuba and for the murder of Tomas Enrique de Rosa.'

Pauline rolled up the paper then handed it back to Ermano with shaking hands. She did not love Tomas but he was still her father. Dominic came to her side.

"I'm sorry, Paulina. We can postpone the attack if you wish."

"No," Pauline said. "We proceed as plan. Just give me a moment."

"As you wish," Dominic replied.

Dominic and Ermano left the cave section. Pauline's eyes glistened. Another person was dead because of her. True, both had volunteered to help her knowing the consequences but that did not make the guilt easier to bear. Gonzales was personally responsible. She would make him pay.

* * *

La Hacienda loomed as a grotesque sore surrounded by the island's natural beauty. Situated on the edge of the tropical forest, it had once been the site of a large manor, hence its name. The owner was long dead and forgotten to history, but the remains of his homestead served as the foundation of the prison. It was not Cuba's most notorious prison, but it was its most known and most despised.

Much care was taken to make sure *La Hacienda* was inescapable. Spikes crowned its towering walls; the windows were narrow slits cut into the stone, which rendered the cells unbearably hot. If an inmate somehow managed to breach its walls he or she would have to cross an open field one hundred yards wide before encountering a thorn bush filled moat. Diablos patrolled the open area, steam drifting from their exhaust pipes as their turrets pivoted from side to side scanning the open ground.

A rumbling captured the Diablos' attention and the turrets twisted in the direction of the single lane road leading to the gates. A prison wagon jostled over the uneven asphalt, carrying its most recent load of miscreants. Inside the wagon the serious looks on the faces of its captives reflected their mood. The drivers were just as focused, their eyes locked on the road ahead. As they neared the moat the driver honked the horn. The gate opened and a massive treaded vehicle drove through. It was a rolling gate, a lumbering vehicle carrying the only access to the prison. The wagon reached the moat then came to a stop. One of the drivers peered through the viewport into the back of the prison wagon.

"You all know what to do," Pauline said to her fighters. "Once we're inside, we won't have much time."

The false prisoners nodded then smiled.

She turned to Dominic who sat beside her, uncomfortable in his small uniform.

"You could have found a better fit," he complained.

"It was the best they could do in short notice," she replied. "You shouldn't be so big."

Dominic grinned and Pauline frowned.

"Keep your mind focused on the mission," she said. "No use dreaming of what will never be."

Dominic's smile faded as he turned his head away.

"It's almost here," he said.

The drawbridge truck extended the metal bridge over the moat. Pauline steered the prison wagon over the bridge then stopped beside the vehicle.

"*Hola*!" she shouted. "Can you leave the bridge in place? We won't be long."

The bridge driver, a stern looking man in a worn looking uniform shook his head.

"You know the rules."

Pauline smiled. "Just this once. We won't be long. We'll dump this trash and be on our way."

The stern man slowly smiled. "Okay. Just this once."

Pauline blew him a kiss. "You are so kind."

They drove through the prison gate. The courtyard was empty, the inmates locked down as a new load of prisoners arrived. The guards surrounded the wagon, clubs at the ready. The warden came to the driver's side, tipping her hat to Pauline. She was a medium built woman with tanned brown skin and short cropped hair.

"How many do you have?" she asked.

Pauline lifted her shotgun, the barrel aimed at the warden's chest.

"Enough. Tell your men to put away their clubs and come closer."

The warden wide eyes were locked on Pauline's shotgun.

"Put your clubs away!" she said.

The guards looked puzzled. Pauline tightened her finger on the trigger.

"Put them away!" the warden repeated.

The men hooked their clubs to their belts. The wagon door swung open and the rebels poured out, grabbing the guards then loading them into the wagon.

Pauline exited the wagon, her shotgun still trained on the warden.

"La Rosa," the warden whispered.

Pauline grinned.

"What's your name?" she asked.

"Alegria," she replied.

"Alegria, call in the Diablos," she said.

The warden unclipped the talk box clipped to her shirt pocket.

"Diego, Martinez, I need you inside."

"Yes commander!" the drivers replied.

Pauline nodded to Dominic. He signaled his men and they ran to the gate, taking position on either side. Their goal was to capture the vehicles if possible, destroy them if not.

The Diablos rolled through the gates on their short tracks, the drivers steering them toward the wagon, the gunners leaning on their Gatling guns. Dominic and his men scrambled up the machines like squirrels, catching the drivers unaware. The rebels lifted them and tossed to the ground, the hapless men landing hard on the dirt. Dominic took over the driver's seat of his Diablo then steered it outside the prison, taking position before the gate.

"Okay Alegria," Pauline said. "Let's liberate you prisoners."

Pauline and the others followed Alegria to the warden's office where they confiscated the keys then quickly worked their way through the prison freeing its startled occupants. Pauline waved a short woman with thick hair to her. The woman saluted Pauline as she reached her.

"Yes, La Rosa?"

"Carolina, go to the motor pool and get any vehicles that are operable. We'll fill them up and take everyone with us."

"Some of these people deserve to be here," Carolina warned.

"We'll sort them out later," Pauline replied.

"Take me with you," Alegria blurted.

Pauline frowned. "So you can tell your bosses where we are?"

"No, I would never do that!"

"Sorry, Alegria," Pauline said. "We can't take that chance."

"I can tell you where there are other prisons, secret prisons!" she said.

"Secret prisons?"

Her desperate eyes shifted between Pauline and Carolina. "You have been told that many of your friends are dead. They are not," she said.

Pauline pushed the barrel of her revolver under Alegria's chin. "If you're lying to me, you'll wish I killed you here."

"I am not lying," she said. "I've been a warden for a long time. I've served at every prison in Cuba. I will take you to them. I promise."

"Tie her hands then load her into the wagon," Pauline ordered. "Let's get out of here."

Pauline climbed back into the wagon then followed the commandeered Diablos out of the prison then down the road. She allowed herself a moment of satisfaction. The prison raid had gone much smoother than she anticipated and Alegria would lead them to the other prisons where they would liberate more comrades.

The lead Diablo exploded. Pauline immediately scanned the area and saw nothing. A second explosion caused the second Diablo to veer to the left. Pauline stuck her head out of the window then looked up; three dirigibles glided overhead flying the New Spain flag. She steered the wagon around then sped for the prison, hoping the others would follow her lead. She heard the rattling of Gatling guns; Dominic was apparently laying cover fire. She drove through the gates then slammed on the brakes. The rear door open and the others spilled out. Pauline ran to the rear of the truck. As the others fled Alegria stared at her, a grin on her face.

"Did you actually think I would...?"

Pauline pulled her revolver then shot her in the forehead.

"Adolpho! Miguel!"

Adolpho and Miguel approached, both men carrying heavy sniper rifles purchased with Alejandra's gold.

"Get to the ramparts," Pauline ordered.

She looked to the others. "The rest of you get back inside."

Pauline reached behind the wagon seat then pulled out a long gun case. If there was one thing she learned from Zeke it was that there was no such thing as too many guns. She hurried to the ramparts, keeping low and dodging the lead downpour from the airships. She ducked into one of the storage rooms the opened the gun case. She wasn't as fond of shotguns as Zeke, but there was one variation she thought would be useful. She had a gunsmith make it the moment she settled in Cuba, hoping to use the weapon against the Diablos. The shotgun had an extended barrel with a scope that ran from the stock to the end of the barrel. A loading chamber ran under the barrel. Pauline assembled the gun, loaded it with its special shells, and then continued up the stairs to the ramparts. The gun was heavy; she usually used a bipod to fire it. But she had no time.

"Juarez!" she shouted.

Juarez, one of her men guarding the ramparts, lumbered over to her.

"La Rosa?" he said.

"I need your back," she said with a smile.

Juarez bent over. Pauline dropped the shotgun onto his back then took aim at the closest dirigible.

"Cover your ears," she advised.

Pauline sighted the ship then fired three times. Sparks flashed against the airship before it burst into flames then plummeted to the ground.

She sighted the second dirigible as it turned toward her. Pauline took aim; before she could shoot the dirigible's Gatlings open fire.

"*La Rosa*!" Juarez shouted.

Juarez scrambled to his feet as he knocked Pauline backwards. She yelled as bullets struck her thigh and grazed her shoulder. She looked up to see Juarez shielding her, his eyes clenched as the bullets pummeled his back. For a moment he looked at her and managed to smile, but then his face went slack as he fell on top of her.

Despite the pain in her legs Pauline pulled free of Juarez. She retrieved her gun then propped it on his body. Pauline took aim again at the dirigible as it reloaded then emptied her gun into the ballast. The ship exploded then dropped from the sky. Pauline slumped, weakened by her wounds. Her eyes went to Juarez. There was a slight grin on his face, his eyes staring into the distance.

"Gracias, mi ángel," she whispered.

Pauline crawled to the rampart stairs, dragging her shotgun. Dominic met her.

"Paulina? Oh my God!"

He swept her into his arms then hurried down the stairs.

"Juarez is dead," she said. "He died protecting me. I did not ask him to do that."

"Be quiet," Dominic replied. "We have to get you out of here."

Dominic loaded her into the back of the wagon with the others. Maria Lopez, their field doctor, immediately began dressing her wounds.

"I can't remove the bullets here," she said as she wrapped the wounds. "I can only stop the bleeding. You are lucky."

"No, I was not lucky," Pauline replied. "Juarez was my angel."

The wagon jolted as the engine started. The caravan hurried from La Hacienda, the prison ablaze from the dirigibles' burning remains. Pauline looked at the inferno with mixed emotion. Their mission was complete, but so many died. Was it worth it? She would make sure it was.

- 1 7 -

Zeke peeked through the porthole of his cabin as the cargo ship eased into Havana Harbor. As the whitewashed warehouses and crowded docks came into view, he realized what a big mistake he'd made. He had no connections in Cuba and hadn't taken the time to contact anyone he knew that might. His Spanish was passable at the most.

"Zeke Culpepper, what have you got yourself into?" he whispered.

He had to find Pauline. If he'd taken a little bit more time to prepare himself instead of flying off the handle he'd be in better shape. That's why he tried to keep things on the level. The worst thing in the world was to make serious decisions based on pure emotion.

He shrugged then dressed. Couldn't go back in time; all he could do was move forward through the mess. As he strapped on his guns, someone rapped on his door.

"Mr. Culpepper?"

Zeke grinned as he opened the door. Zenobia walked in with a tray of food.

"Thought you might want something to eat," she said.

"Thank you," Zeke replied.

He sat on his bunk to eat.

"Have some?" he offered.

Zenobia waved her hands. "No thanks. I ate with the crew."

Zeke ate the eggs and bacon then took a sip of the strong sweet coffee.

"This is the best food I've ever had on a ship," he commented.

"That's only because Miss Bedford is on board. Otherwise it would be beans and smoked beef."

"You know, I don't know much about Cuba," he said. "I'm gonna need someone to show me around."

Zenobia grinned. "I was thinking the same thing."

"I'm looking for someone, a person very special to me," Zeke continued. "She's most likely in a lot of trouble with the law here."

"That's half of the people I know," Zenobia replied. "The trouble part at least. I suspect you're going to need somebody who can get you in front of people that can be discreet."

Zeke finished his breakfast then sipped more coffee.

"That's exactly what I need. You volunteering?"

"Not exactly," Zenobia replied. "I don't do nothing for free."

"What about your job here?"

Zenobia shrugged. "Working on this piece of junk ain't ever going to get me where I need to be. You look like a man of means, and I'm sure you're willing to pay good gold to find that lady friend of yours."

"I don't know about gold, but I have eagles," Zeke said.

"Good enough," Zenobia said. "Fifty up front, fifty when we find your lady."

"How do you know I'm looking for a lady?" Zeke said.

Zenobia looked Zeke up and down. "You ain't the kind of man who would take off looking for a friend. Yep, I suspect there's a filly that's got you bucking at the fence."

Zeke reached into his jacket pocket then took out his wallet.

"Twenty up front, twenty when we find my 'filly,'" he said.

"Forty-five," Zenobia replied.

"Twenty-five," Zeke countered.

"Forty or I walk," Zenobia said.

"Thirty or I'll ask you to leave," Zeke said.

"Deal," Zenobia replied.

Zeke handed the eagles to Zenobia. She took the bills, counted them, and then stuffed them into her pocket.

"Meet me on deck in thirty minutes," Zenobia said.

"Will do," Zeke replied.

Zenobia opened the door to a startled Catherine.

"Zenobia? What are you doing here?"

"Business," Zenobia said. "By the way, Miss Catherine, I quit."

Catherine watched Zenobia walk away, her mouth agape. When she turned to face Zeke, her expression was not pleasant.

"Mr. Culpepper, what have you done?"

"I apologize, Miss Catherine," Zeke said. "But I needed someone to get me around this city."

"You could have asked me!" she replied. "I'm well-connected."

"The people you know are the people I need to avoid," Zeke said. "This is dirty work."

"Like your work in Savannah?"

Zeke smirked. "Kind of."

Zeke tipped his hat then worked his way past Catherine into the hallway.

"Thank you for the ride," he said. "And I appreciate all you've done."

He handed Catherine a leather pouch; she opened the pouch and her eyes went wide.

"Thank you, Mr. Culpepper!"

"I hope I can hitch a ride back if you're docked when I'm done with my business."

"We'll be docked for two weeks," Catherine said. "And don't bring any trouble back with you."

"I can't promise I won't," Zeke said. "But I'll try not to."

When Zeke reached the deck, Zenobia was nowhere to be found. For a minute he thought he might be a scam victim but the woman finally arrived, accompanied by tall, ebony man with thick arms and a sour look. His bald head was covered with tattoos.

"I didn't know you were bringing friends," Zeke commented.

"This is Coot," Zenobia said.

Zeke and Coot shook, Zeke flinching as the man squeezed the blood out of his hand.

"Please to meet you, boss," Coot said.

Zeke shook the feeling back into his hand. "Something tells me Coot ain't your real name."

The man grin looked menacing. "Coot is good enough."

"Coot's Spanish is better than mine," Zenobia said. "It's also easier to get folks to talk when he's on your side. Less folks get shot that way."

Zenobia's last statement was meant for Zeke.

"I ain't never shot a person that didn't deserve to be shot," Zeke replied. "I pride myself on that."

Zenobia smiled. "Come on. Coot's got a good place to start."

Custom officers waited at the end of the docks to check everyone's papers. Zeke took the time during the trip to secure the proper documents. The customs officer scrutinized his documents longer than Zenobia's and Coot; when he looked up his face was not pleasant.

"Ezekiel Culpepper," the man stated.

"Yes, sir," Zeke replied.

The customs officer's face twisted as if he'd swallowed bad pork. "A Freedonian."

"Yes, sir," Zeke replied.

"What is your business in Cuba?"

"I'm thinking about getting into the cigar business," Zeke replied. "Cuba's the best place to start."

"Open your bags," the man said.

Zenobia stepped between Zeke and the officer.

"Is that really necessary?" She reached out to shake the officer's hand, a twenty in her palm. The officer shook her hand, taking the twenty.

"Welcome to Cuba, *Senor* Culpepper," he said.

The trio hurried away from the docks.

"I don't pay bribes," Zeke said.

"I do," Zenobia answered. "And I expect you to pay me back."

"That could have gone either way," he said.

"Coot knew him," Zenobia replied. "We were lucky to get him. With all that hardware you're carrying we would have been stuck in customs for days."

"Doesn't seem right," Zeke commented.

Zenobia stopped walking.

"Look, you paid me to help you find your sweetheart. Let me do my job."

Zeke shrugged. "Okay then. It's your show."

Zenobia smiled. "Thank you."

They walked toward the city.

"So where do we start?" Zeke asked.

"Coot knows a place where we can get good information. Nobody enters Cuba without being noticed. The government is very nervous. It is also very corrupt."

"Sounds familiar," Zeke replied.

He followed his guides through the Havana streets, making mental notes of their directions and the surroundings.

"We're here," Coot said.

'Here' was a narrow street crammed with small shops and hawkers. The sounds of drums pulsated through the humid air, blending with a myriad of voices. Despite his breakfast Zeke's stomach grumbled as they worked their way through the throng and past the various food vendors. The press slackened neared a shop front framed by two hulking men dressed in white vest exposing their torsos and white pants gathered at their waists with blue cotton sashes. The sashes held machetes. The men eyed them as they approached, their scrutiny lessening when Coot took the lead.

"*Que pasa,*" he said.

"*Nada,*" the men replied in unison.

They hugged and shook hands.

"Where have you been hiding?" one of the men said to Coot.

"I work on a cargo ship now, Cedro," Coot replied.

"That must be boring as shit," the other man said.

They laughed.

"Yes, Jair it's boring, but it's safer," Coot answered.

"We could use you," Cedro said. The look on his face suggested his statement carried a double meeting.

Coot rubbed his chin. "We'll talk later. Right now, I'd like you to meet my friends Zenobia and Zeke."

The men's suspicious gaze returned.

"They're Freedonians," Coot said.

"What would rich Freedonians want with us?" Cedro said.

"Zeke is looking for someone," Coot said.

The duo's expression went from suspicious to hostile. They pushed past Coot, striding directly to Zenobia and Zeke. Zeke's right hand disappeared into his jacket.

"No!" Zenobia whispered. "Let Coot handle this."

"He doesn't seem to be doing a good job," Zeke replied.

"Who are you looking for, Freedonian?" Jair asked.

"A woman," Zeke replied. He decided to be honest. "She was brought here against her will. I've come to take her back."

"What is her name?" Cedro asked.

"Pauline Rose," Zeke replied.

The men pulled their machetes. Coot grabbed Cedro's shoulders then spun him around. He planted a perfect right cross on the man's jaw that sent him to the ground unconscious. Jair was advancing on Zeke and Zenobia, his machete drawn. Zeke whipped out his shotgun.

"Hold that pose, partner," he said.

Jair froze, a snarl on his face.

"You will never take *La Rosa*!" Jair shouted.

Coot turned Jair about and repeated his knockout move. He glared at Zeke.

"Let's get out of here now!" he said.

Coot ran; Zeke and Zenobia followed. They ran until they were clear of the cluttered market and in open ground. When they stopped Coot reached into his pants pocket and took out the money Zenobia had given to him. He grabbed her wrist then shoved the eagles into her palm.

"I'm done," he said. "I want no part of this!"

"Wait a minute," Zeke said. "What the hell is going on?"

Coot turned to Zeke.

"If I had known you were looking for *La Rosa*, I would have never signed on."

"I ain't looking for no *La Rosa*," Zeke said. "I'm looking for Pauline Rose!"

Coot rolled his eyes. "Fool, Pauline Rose is *La Rosa*!"

Zeke stood confused.

"And who the hell is *La Rosa*?" he shouted.

"She's a legend," Zenobia said. "About ten years ago, the workers revolted. They were led by *El Cinco*, 'The Five.' Paulina de Rosa was the most admired of them all."

"Pauline," Zeke whispered.

"And now she's back and the revolution has begun again," Coot said. "The government is hunting her, and you look like government."

Their conversation was interrupted by whistle.

"Run!" Coot said. "Back to the ship!"

Coot sprinted down the street, Zeke and Zenobia close behind. They turned down the street and met a wall of soldiers and police. Zeke back pedaled then ran in the other direction.

"*Alto! Alto!*" the authorities shouted.

Zeke and Zenobia caught up with Coot.

"How do we get to the Freedonian embassy?" Zeke shouted between breaths.

"This way!" Coot shouted back.

Coot took a right turn down another alley. They were making great progress before running into another group of policemen.

"Is this the only way?" Zeke asked.

"Yeah," Coot replied.

Zeke tucked his cross into his shirt.

"Lord forgive me," he whispered.

Zeke whipped out his shotgun and fired low. The policemen tumbled to the ground clutching their wounded legs. He didn't have to say anything; Coot and Zenobia ran and leapt over the writhing officers. Zeke did the same. He was mid-air when he jerked then fell on the pile. One of the officers held him by the ankle; the others grabbed him and battered him with open hands and fists. Zeke kicked and flailed the best he could to free himself but more policemen arrived. They yelled and cursed in Spanish, hitting Zeke over and over with their clubs. Pain overwhelmed him as he slipped into darkness.

* * *

Zeke awoke tied to a chair in an empty room. He ached everywhere, especially over his right eye. He instinctively attempted to touch the wound but ropes held his hands. He winced as he raised his head. The room smelled of urine and blood stains covered the stone floor and walls.

"This ain't good," he whispered. "Ain't good at all."

The sound of latches opening echoed through the room. The door swung open and two uniformed men marched up to him. One of the men grabbed his chin then lifted his head.

"*Es el,*" the man said. He let go of Zeke's chin then slapped him before leaving the room.

"You're gonna pay for that," Zeke said.

"You are in no position to issue threats, Ezekiel Culpepper," the other man said.

Zeke looked at the man. "You know me, but I don't know you."

"No, you don't," the man said. "But we have someone in common. Paulina de Rosa."

As much as he loved her, Zeke was beginning to rue the day he met Pauline.

"That man who slapped you. You killed his friends."

Zeke's eyes widened.

"Yes, that was us," the man said.

"Looks like you got what you wanted," Zeke said.

The man frowned. "Not exactly."

"It's got nothing to do with me," Zeke said. "I'm here to settle things."

The man grinned. "I think you're here to help her."

Zeke laughed. "Now why on God's green earth would I want to do that? I thought I was marrying a hard-working farm woman. I had no idea she was a wanted rebel. I'm a bounty hunter. I don't want anything to do with anyone living a bad life. I came here to let her know that."

"A letter would have been more convenient," the man said. "But I'll give you the benefit of doubt. I believe I can arrange that meeting. Julio!"

Another man entered the room carrying a daguerreotype mounted on a tripod. He set up the camera, and then approached Zeke.

"Please sit up and remain still," the man said.

Zeke did as he was told, managing to smile despite his injuries. The photography took several minutes; the man inspected the image then left the room.

"So how to you expect to get that to Pauline when I suspect you have no idea where she is?" Zeke asked.

"*La Rosa* has eyes everywhere," the man replied. "She will see your tintype and receive our message."

He approached Zeke. Zeke prepared himself for a thrashing. Instead the man untied his ropes.

"We'll transfer you to more comfortable accommodations," the man said.

Zeke rubbed his wrists. "I'd appreciate it more if you'd just let me go."

"It's up to Paulina when or if that happens," the man replied. "Until then, enjoy your stay, Señor Culpepper."

The man knocked on the door. It opened and he walked out; another guard led Zeke to a cell with a bed, sink and toilet.

"Much better," Zeke joked.

He sat on the bed. The guard handed him a bowl of some type of cereal that despite its bland taste satisfied his hunger.

"Alright Miss Rose," Zeke said. "This all better be worth it. It sure better be."

- 1 8 -

The train eased into Camaguey station on a sunny afternoon, a light breeze rustling the nearby pines and teasing the palmettos. The porters placed the steps for departure at the first-class car exit, sparing no luxury for the wealthy passengers who often visited the city for its unique culture and the beauty of the nearby archipelago. Most of the passengers were couples traveling together, but one passenger had come alone. Her beauty and outgoing nature drew the attention of all on board and won her invitations to share a few days with many of them, but she politely refused. Though her manner and dress suggested someone eager for a few days' rest, her purpose was far from such intentions.

Alejandra shielded her eyes from the bright sun with a gloved hand before raising her parasol. She scanned the city then looked in the direction of the islands. When she received the note from Paulina explaining what her father had shared Alejandra was immediately suspicious. Tomas was well connected, but no one in his circle would have access to military information, especially that of a secret nature. Her husband Antonio was a different matter. He was constantly in the company of the Spanish generals, and during their frequent smoking and drinking a few were bound to spill secrets. There was mention of the warship project, but none of those conversations pointed to the Camaguey archipelago. Alejandra suspected something else was afoot and she had come herself to be certain.

Her wagon appeared minutes later, the driver a handsome young local wearing a loose cotton shirt and pants that ended at his calves. A wide brim straw hat fell to his eyebrows; his tanned face disappeared as he nodded his head.

"*Senora* Alejandra?" he said.

"Yes?"

"I am Enrique Ponciano," the young man said. "My boss sent me to pick you up."

"How kind of him," she said.

"Not so kind," Enrique said. "You paid for it."

Alejandra laughed. "Aren't you the honest one."

Enrico smiled. "Yes I am. And let me honestly say that you are a beautiful woman."

"Too many men have said that before you," she answered. "I challenge you to say something more original before my visit comes to an end."

"Your challenge is accepted," Enrique said. "But since I'll need some time to think of such a platitude, I will sing to you instead."

"Have I paid for that as well?" Alejandra asked.

"Yes, you have, *Senora*. Yes, you have."

Enrique loaded her luggage then they were off to the coast. As he promised Enrique sang as they traveled. His voice was extraordinary. The time melted away due to his melodious songs. They finally reached her destination, a quaint cottage within view of the pristine beaches. Enrique jumped from the wagon, gathered her possessions then delivered them to the cottage porch, not missing a note. When he finished his song, Alejandra applauded.

"You should be performing in Havana," she said.

Enrique shook his head.

"I am but a simple man," he said. "Work is hard but it is honest. I hear being an artist in such a big city can be treacherous."

"That is true," Alejandra replied. "However, if you ever decide to do so please let me know. I would be an eager patron."

"See, you are truly beautiful!" Enrique said. "My wife and I reside in the next cottage. We will bring you breakfast in the morning and change your linen each night."

"I prefer to take care of myself," Alejandra replied. "But don't worry. It will not decrease my payment or my tips."

"As you wish, *Senora*. I will make sure that if I choose to sing at night, I will do so loud enough for you to hear."

"I will hold you to that," she said. "One more thing, Enrique. Where can I rent a good horse?"

"Senor Martinez has a few," the young man replied. "I'll fetch you one today. It will be waiting for you tomorrow morning."

"Excellent!" Alejandra gave Enrique a sizable tip then entered the cabin.

She settled in, changing from her traveling clothes into a pair of pants, sandals and a loose cotton shirt. She walked to the beach, strolling along the sandy expanse as if enjoying the time alone. In reality she gazed toward the supposed location of the hidden ship hoping to spy some indication of its presence. Once she was far enough away from the cottage, she took out a pair of binoculars and scanned the distance, searching for any sign of a large ship. After a few moments she relented.

"Alé, you are such a fool," she said aloud to herself. A secret ship would not sit in the open for everyone to see, even in the Camaguey archipelago. She would have to go for a ride and search the area. Tonight, she would settle into her little *hacienda* and pretend to be on a respite.

The morning came with bright sun, a gentle breeze and tapping on the front door. Alejandra rose, put on her house robe and rubbed her eyes as she stumbled to the door. She opened it to a petite young woman with a demure smile. The woman held a tray with breakfast and coffee.

"*Buenos dias*, Senora," she said. "I am Luciana."

"*Buenos dias*. I suspect you are Enrique's wife?"

Luciana smiled. "Yes I am. I have come with your breakfast. May I come in?"

"Of course."

Alejandra stepped aside and Luciana entered. She tipped to the table then laid out the breakfast, placing each plate and cup with practiced precision. Alejandra sat at the table and Luciana began to serve her. Alejandra waved her away.

"Sit," she said. "Have breakfast with me."

Luciana looked surprised. "No, *Senora*. It is not allowed."

"It is today," Alejandra said. "I insist. Besides, who will know you broke the rules. I certainly won't tell."

Luciana looked about as if she was being watched.

"It's not enough for two," she finally said.

"We'll share. I don't each much and you have probably eaten earlier. I'd love the company."

Luciana looked about one more time before smiling then sitting. Alejandra took her knife and fork and divided the food, arranging it on opposite sides of the plates.

"I'm afraid we'll have to drink the juice and coffee from the same glass," Alejandra said. "I hope you don't mind."

Luciana smiled as she shook her head. Alejandra cut her eggs and began to eat. Luciana followed suit.

"Is Camaguey your home?" Alejandra asked.

"Yes, *Senora*," Luciana replied. "I have lived here all my life.

"Call me Alé," Alejandra said. "You and Enrique make a good couple."

Luciana laughed then covered her mouth. "*Gracias.*"

"Does it bother you that he flirts with the guests?"

Luciana shook her head as she ate. "No, *Senora* . . . I mean Alé. Enrique is a very good man. I have known him all my life. He does what he has to do to make money. Flirting brings in bigger tips. Besides, he would never cheat on me. He drank from my tinajón."

"That sounds deliciously scandalous," Alejandra replied.

Luciana laughed. "I can assure you it is not, Señora. That is a tinajón."

She pointed at the clay pot in the cottage garden.

"It is said that if a man drinks from a woman's tinajón he will stay with her forever. I don't believe such things, but it is good conversation."

Alejandra sipped her coffee. "It is. However, I prefer my insinuation. You seem very confident about his loyalty," Alejandra said.

"I am," Luciana replied. "He also knows that if he cheated on me and I discovered it I would kill him."

There was no humor in Luciana's voice when she uttered those words. Alejandra was impressed.

"Yes, I believe you would."

Luciana seemed relaxed, so Alejandra decided to get to the real reason she asked the young lady to have breakfast with her.

"I suspect you do not get many visitors like me," she said.

"No, we don't. Mostly foreigners come to fish or look at the islands. But a few weeks ago, the soldiers came."

"Soldiers?" Alejandra feigned shock. "Why would soldiers come here?"

Luciana looked about again then leaned close to Alejandra.

"I hear that *La Rosa* has returned and revived the revolution. The Spanish know that many rebels come from Camaguey so I think they have come to make sure it doesn't happen again."

"Where are they?" Alejandra asked.

"They built a camp about five miles north. They do not come into the city. They keep to themselves. Their supplies come from their ships."

"How do you know this?"

"Enrique rode to the camp hoping to sell them some souvenirs," Luciana said. "They were very angry and began shooting at him. I was so upset with him! I told him not to go."

"I'm glad he is safe," Alejandra said.

"*Gracias*, Alé."

Alejandra steered the conversation to more mundane things. She'd learned what she needed to know. Still, she would have to ride out to the camp to see if the ship was there. They finished breakfast and Luciana cleared the table, stacking the plates on the tray. As she stepped through the door Enrique rode up on a donkey, holding the reins of a fine stallion. A wide smile came to her face. This wonderful beast would do nicely.

"*Hola, Senora*!" he shouted. "I see you have met my beautiful wife."

Alejandra and Luciana walked down the steps together.

"Yes, I have," she said. "You are lucky to have her."

"I know." Enrique took the tray from Luciana then kissed her.

"Enrique!" she said.

Enrique laughed. "My wife is very shy. She doesn't like it when I kiss her in public. But in private she is a lioness."

Luciana punched Enrique's shoulder.

"Don't share our private business! Alé did not come here to hear such things."

Enrique's eyes widened. "Alé? You two are using nicknames now?"

"Be quiet and take me home," Luciana said.

Alejandra laughed then went to inspect the horse.

"This is a lovely animal," she said.

"You know horses, *Senora*?" Enrique asked.

"I do. I own quite a few." Alejandra took a look at the saddle as well and smirked.

"A good saddle as well. I see you pay close attention to details. This is excellent for a rider with ample hips."

Enrique blushed. “What can I say?”

He helped Luciana into the wagon.

“Enjoy your ride, *Senora*. What time should we expect you back?”

“At sunset,” she said.

“We will see you tonight then,” Enrique said. “*Adios, Senora*!”

The happy couple rode away. Alejandra waited until they were over the horizon before going back inside. She grabbed her pack, which included a canteen, pistol, machete and a change of clothes. She loaded her horse, mounted then rode north to the location of the camp. The trip took her longer than she expected; it was well past noon before she spotted signs of the base. Alejandra dismounted, changed into her Mambises uniform then continued on foot, hoping that her horse had the discipline to stay nearby. The encampment finally came into focus. To her dismay the soldiers built a wall which blocked her view of the harbor. She could see the masts of ships rising over the wall but she needed better confirmation. She had no idea how this secret ship would look but she was sure it would be much different than what she was familiar with. There was no choice; she had to get inside.

Alejandra crept around the perimeter, studying the wall closely. She finally found the weak spot she searched for; a gap created by a tidal creek which flowed into the ocean. Either the soldiers were too lazy to make the extra effort to build over the creek or they thought the creek itself was deterrent enough. In both cases they were wrong.

Alejandra waded into the warm water. It was deeper than she expected, forcing her to swim between the banks. She quickly made her way to the sandy bank then slipped into the nearby bush. She took out her binoculars then scrutinized the harbor. There were a few cargo ships, but nothing that resembles a warship. There were however many soldiers. The letter was a ruse; whoever sent it expected the rebels to come in force and they would be ready. She'd seen all she needed to see. It was time to go back to the cottage.

"*Alto*!"

Alejandra reacted instinctively, spinning toward the sound as she threw her machete. The blade sank into the chest of the startled soldier; he blinked before collapsing to the ground. Alejandra ran to the man then extracted the blade. No sooner did she do so she was struck across the jaw by something hard. She fell onto her back, losing the machete. She shook her head then opened her eyes to see another soldier standing over her, his rifle aimed at her head. He was opening his mouth to call out when Alejandra yanked off her hat, her hair cascading about her shoulders. The soldier gasped and lowered his weapon; Alejandra kicked his feet from under him and he fell on top of her. She pushed him over onto his back then snatched his knife from his sheath. She covered the man's mouth as she stabbed him in the throat, pressing down on his mouth until he ceased moving. She stood, her jaw sore and her clothes covered with blood. She took a quick look about and saw no one else. Running as fast as she could she eased into the creek then swam to the other side. Making sure there were no other soldiers about she hurried back to where she left the horse. The beast had wandered away, so she did the only thing she could do. She found a clump of thick shrubs, curled up as best she could then attempted to sleep.

Alejandra awoke the next morning to the gentle nudging of her errant horse. She rose slowly then mounted the horse, kicking it partly in anger but mostly to speed him on his way. The horse seemed to sense her urgency; it galloped the entire way back to the cottage. When they arrived Luciana's wagon was hitched outside. By now the woman would know Alejandra had not spent the night in the cottage. When she emerged through the front door her expression conveyed her relief.

"You are safe!" Luciana exclaimed.

Alejandra climbed down from the horse. Luciana ran up to her. She looked at her and blanched upon seeing Alejandra's blood-stained clothes. She grabbed Alejandra's arm then dragged her into the house.

"You must change quickly!" she said.

"What is going on?" Alejandra asked.

"Two soldiers were killed last night," Luciana said. She looked at the machete hanging from Alejandra's waist and her bruised jaw.

"The soldiers think rebels are afoot," she continued. "They are searching every house in the city. They will be here soon. Comandante Guillermo Fuentes is leading the search personally."

Alejandra grinned. "We can take our time then. There is no hurry."

"Pardon me Alé, but it is obvious you killed those men," Luciana said. "You are a Mambises."

"Yes, I am," Alejandra admitted.

"The soldiers can't see you like this. They will know it was you."

"There's a difference between knowing something and being able to do something about it," Alejandra said. "Please tend to breakfast. We will share like we did yesterday. But let's eat on the porch. It's a warm morning and I'd like to enjoy it."

Luciana looked puzzled but did as Alejandra asked. Alejandra changed into something more suitable then applied make-up to hide her bruise. She stashed her Mambises uniform and machete, and then went to the porch. The sound of hoof beats drew her attention. The comandante and his men were riding to the cottage. Luciana waited, her expression uneasy. Alejandra approached the table then placed a gentle hand on Luciana's shoulder.

"Stay calm," Alejandra said. "Let me handle this."

Alejandra sat then began eating her meal. Luciana took one more glance at the soldiers before doing the same.

The riders dismounted then marched to the porch. The comandante climbed the stairs, leaving his men behind.

"*Senora*," he said. "We have come here on a matter of grave importance."

Alejandra raised her head, exposing her face.

"Is that you Guillermo?" she said. "What a pleasant surprise!"

"What...*Senora* Espinoza! What are you doing here?"

"Taking some time to explore your wonderful islands," Alejandra replied as she extended her hand. "How are you and your family?"

Guillermo took her hand then kissed it. "They are well, *Senora*. I take it you have enjoyed your visit?"

"Very much," Alejandra answered. "Luciana and her husband have been very attentive."

Guillermo's polite expression faded. "I'm sorry to inconvenience you, but we had a serious incident at the army camp last night. Two of our men were killed. We suspect *La Rosa* may be in the area. We would like to question your servants."

"That won't be necessary," Alejandra replied. "I can vouch for their whereabouts."

"That may be true," Guillermo said. "But they may have other information that could help us."

Alejandra sighed. "So, you have come to ruin my *siesta*."

"No *Senora*, that is not my intention."

"I think so Guillermo. If you take them away and interrogate them, they will be in a sour mood afterwards. Can't you make an exception?"

Guillermo worked his chin with his gloved hand.

"If I do so, will you make sure your husband shares with me his finest rum on my next visit?"

Alejandra laughed. "Of course. Antonio will be vexed, but he will do as I ask."

Guillermo grinned. "Then we will bother you no further. Enjoy your stay. Be sure to visit before you leave."

"I will," Alejandra said.

The soldiers mounted then rode on their way. As soon as they were out of sight. Luciana grasped her hands then kissed them.

"Thank you, Alé," Luciana said. "God bless you!The comandante can be quite harsh."

"You are safe," Alejandra said. "Now let's enjoy the rest of this wonderful breakfast before it gets cold."

Alejandra kept her aloof façade as she ate, but her mind mulled over her situation. The secret harbor was a trap. She would have to tell Paulina, but she would wait a few days so her departure would not seem suspicious. For now, she would have to be what she pretended to be, a woman of means on a sabbatical. She hoped Paulina would be patient. There was nothing else she could do.

- 19 -

A crescent moon hung like a luminous ornament in the clear night sky over the city of Matanzas and its peaceful harbor. Gas lights flickered on the narrow streets, illuminating the jewel of northern Cuba. The cultural center of the island, Matanzas was the epicenter of Afro-Cuban culture. It was also firmly controlled by the rebels led by Paulina de Rosa.

Pauline looked out on the harbor from the church tower, surrounded by her officers. There were others present as well. The *Abakua* had come to her weeks ago. The secret fraternity sent a messenger before their arrival, sharing information she hoped would be true. They would know soon.

"There," Dominic said as he pointed toward the horizon.

Pauline looked where Dominic pointed.

"I don't see . . ."

The light flickered like a spark.

An elderly man standing close to her touched her shoulder.

"I told you he would come," the man said.

Pauline looked down at the man them smiled.

"Yes, you did, Alonzo," she replied. "Come, let us greet our *compañeros*."

They descended to the street then loaded into the truck waiting for them. Pauline grew nervous as they approached the harbor. It had been ten years since she'd seen him. She had no idea how she would react.

They reached the harbor as the fishing boat ran aground. Five men climbed out then waded through the surf. Two of the men carried rifles. Dominic walked beside Pauline, a kerosene lamp in his hand. As they neared the men Pauline smiled. The man who drew her attention smiled as well. They walked to each other then embraced.

"Antonio," Pauline whispered.

"*La Rosa*," Antonio Maceo replied.

She held him a moment longer then stood back to take stock of the man who was once a close companion. He still wore his beard, his hair cut short as well.

"You haven't aged a day," she said.

"And you are still as lovely as your name," Antonio replied.

Another man stepped into the light, a man Pauline respected as much as Antonio.

"Quintin," Pauline said. "The rumors were that you were dead."

"You know rumors," Quintin said.

Pauline hugged her old friend as well.

"I assume it was you who contacted the *Abakua*?" Pauline asked.

Quintin nodded. "We were excited when we heard you had returned. We have been waiting for this moment for a long time."

"I'm happy you are here," Pauline said. "Very happy."

"Where is Angelo?" Antonio asked.

"Angelo is dead," Pauline answered. "He died of the flu."

"I am so sorry," Antonio said. "You two were very close."

"And who is this man?" Quintin asked.

"Dominic Valdez," Pauline said.

"Ah, the Freedonian spy," Antonio said.

Dominic's eyes went wide as Pauline laughed.

"Yes, he works for the Freedonians. But they have been useful."

"And they will continue to be until they get what they want," Quintin said.

"What do you want, Freedonian?" Antonio asked.

"I am not Freedonian!" Dominic said. "I am as Cuban as you."

"A man takes the nationality of the master he serves," Antonio said.

"I don't have to listen to this!"

Dominic stomped away.

"That was cruel," Pauline said.

"But necessary," Antonio replied. "And what about you Paulina? Who do you serve?"

"You have no right to question me, Antonio," Pauline replied. "You more than anyone know where I stand. The Freedonians are not like the Americans. They support the freedom of African people around the world. They are not concerned with keeping the status quo."

"It's not like you came on your own," Antonio replied. "If not for the Freedonians neither of us would stand here today."

"I would not," Pauline said. "But now that we are here there is much work to do."

Pauline gestured toward the city. "Come. We have food waiting. Once you've rested, we can discuss details."

They climbed into the truck then rode back to the city museum, their current headquarters. As they exited the truck Ramirez, one of Pauline's messengers, rushed to her side.

"*La Rosa*!" he shouted. "You must see this!"

The boy grasped Pauline by the wrist and put a folded piece of paper into her hand. She looked at Ramirez puzzled as she unfolded the paper. What she saw made her gasp.

Dear La Rosa,

It seems I've found something that belongs to you. I would love to meet with you and discuss it in more detail. Please do not keep me waiting. I'm not sure how long I can keep it before it becomes lost forever.

General Gomez

Pauline stared at the picture of Zeke, a shocked look on her face. Antonio came to her side then removed the note from her hand.

"Who is this?" he asked.

"Zeke Culpepper," Pauline replied. "Someone very dear to me who shouldn't be here."

"Another Freedonian?" Antonio said. "These people are causing more trouble than they are worth."

Pauline strode to Dominic.

"Dominic, where would Gonzales most likely keep a secret prisoner?"

"I'm not sure," Dominic said. "Are you thinking of actually meeting with them?"

"I have no choice," she replied. "They'll kill him."

"You cannot jeopardize the revolution, La Rosa," Antonio said. "Nothing comes before it. If your lover must suffer the ultimate price then so be it."

"I'm not here for the revolution," Pauline said. "I'm here because the Freedonians gave me up to do a job for them. This uprising is cover for them to destroy a secret weapon. Now they've dragged Zeke into it."

"What weapon?" Antonio asked.

"Dominic can answer that better than I can," Pauline said.

Antonio and Quintin turned to Dominic.

"The Freedonians believe New Spain is developing some type of super ship that would break their domination over the South Atlantic. Their plan was to spark a new revolution as a cover to find and destroy this ship if it exists. If we accomplished this, the Freedonians would send military aid and cut off supplies to Cuba from New Spain."

"And do you know, if the ship exists, where it would be located?"

Dominic frowned. "No. We have scoured Cuba and found no signs of it. We have questioned all the workers employed by the Spaniards and still nothing."

"I receive a message from Alé," Pauline said. "We heard the ship might be in Camaguey but it was a set up."

"Then it is obvious the ship is not in Cuba," Antonio said. "But I'm sure it is not far away."

"Where could it be?" Dominic asked.

The answer struck Pauline like a lightning bolt and she smiled.

"The one place we would never look, for it is the one place we would never go. *Isla de la Juventud*," Pauline said.

Antonio smiled. "Brilliant."

"We should gather a force and go their immediately," Dominic said.

"No," Pauline said. "I have to free Zeke."

Antonio frowned at both of them. "Nothing comes before the revolution."

"There is a way all can be satisfied," Pauline said. "But it will require patience, daring and coordination."

"We're listening," Antonio said.

"Then gather around," Pauline said. "And let's share secrets.

- 20 -

General Gonzales was sitting on the veranda of his hacienda enjoying a leisurely breakfast when the letter arrived. His servant cleared his throat for the General's attention.

"What is it, Javier?"

"Señor Gonzales, this arrived for you this morning."

Javier extended a silver plate with a folded note resting on the polished surface. Gonzales took the note, opened it gingerly then read it.

Gonzales,
Keep him.
La Rosa

A smirk came to Gonzales's face, hiding his frustration. He was sure the threat to do harm to her lover would bring her out, but apparently the man meant nothing to her despite what he'd been led to believe. The only thing left to do was kill the man and get back to the business of finding La Rosa among the rabble.

He tore up the note.

"Burn it," he said, "then bring me my horse."

Gonzales finished his breakfast as he waited for his horse. The first thing he would do was kill this Zeke Culpepper. Even if *La Rosa* didn't care about him, at least she would know he was a man of his word. It helped that the Freedonian had entered the country unknown. He wouldn't have to explain the death of a Freedonian citizen to their ambassador. This situation could be handled neatly and unnoticed.

Javier arrived with his horse and he set out to where the Freedonian was being held. No reason to put off the inevitable; the sooner the man was dead the sooner he could get back to hunting *La Rosa*. The ride to the secret prison took most of the day mainly due to the ruggedness of the trail which branched off the main road. The pathway eventually widened into a clearing which held a small windowless house. Two guards sat in chairs on either side of the entrance. They stood at attention as Gonzales entered the clearing. As the general dismounted the guard on the right unlocked the door then opened it. The stench met Gonzales and he took out his handkerchief, covering his mouth and nose. Zeke Culpepper sat on the floor, his back against the wall, his arms resting on his knees. He managed to smile as Gonzales approached.

"How you doing, general?" Zeke asked. "Or should I say, *'Como estas?'*"

"I see your Spanish is improving," Gonzales said. "Too bad you won't have much use for it."

Zeke's smile wavered for a moment then returned.

"I guess I'll be going home then," he said.

"Not exactly," Gonzales replied. "I received a note this morning from your *senorita*. I'm afraid it was bad news. She said, and these are her exact words, 'Keep him.'"

Zeke shrugged. "I guess she didn't love me as much as I thought."

The Freedonian tilted his head to the side.

"Tell me, how are going to do this?" he asked. "I'd prefer a bullet to the head. That's the best way to go."

"No, *Señor* Culpepper, that would be too easy," Gonzales said. "I suspect *La Rosa* cares for you more than she lets on. Like most revolutionaries she believes the cause is more important than anything. But I think once she finds your mutilated body, she will not think so much of the cause."

"You think killing me will weaken her," Zeke said.

"Yes," Gonzales answered.

Zeke laughed. "Well mister, I can see you don't know Pauline –excuse me, *La Rosa*very well."

Gonzales frowned.

"Your pathetic bravado is entertaining, but I have more pressing matters to attend to."

"I guess you won't be the person dealing out the punishment," Zeke said. "I didn't think you were the torturing kind. Didn't think you had the stomach for it. Seems I was right."

"Goodbye, Zeke Culpepper," Gonzales said. "May your soul burn in Hell."

Zeke nodded his head. "See you soon."

Gonzales hurried from the building. He waited for the guards to close and lock the door before issuing his orders.

"Use machetes" he said. He marched to his horse, mounted, and then disappeared into the thicket.

* * *

Zeke's smile faded as soon as the door closed behind Gonzales.

So, she said 'keep him,' he thought. Under any other circumstances he would be sure Pauline was bluffing. But in Cuba he couldn't be sure. He was still trying to digest the fact that his fiancé was a major leader in the Cuban revolution that took place over ten years ago. It took a certain type of person to be a wartime leader, a person accustomed to making decisions that costs lives in order to achieve the greater good. If what Gonzales said was true, Pauline chose the revolution.

Zeke waited for his moment of truth. He had not been fed, which wasn't any different than the other ten days he'd been in custody. It was hard to know exactly, but he guessed by what little light seeping through cracks in the plank wood walls that darkness was approaching. Zeke attempted to stay alert but fatigue and hunger took its toll. As the last light of day ducked under the pines Zeke was startled awake by a commotion outside the door. He prepared himself for his fate as he listened to the jangling keys and the squealing of the opening door. A man stepped inside, but he was not one of Zeke's captors. This man wore clothes that seemed to be a uniform, khaki pants and shirt with a straw hat. He carried a bloody machete in his right hand.

"*Señor* Culpepper?" the man asked in heavily accented English.

"That'd be me," Zeke replied. He stood as he sized the man up. Zeke was weak, but he figured he could take the man if he timed his attack just right.

The man smiled. "You come with me. *La Rosa* will be happy to see you."

"*La Rosa*? You mean Pauline? Pauline sent you?"

"*Si*," the man said. "You come quickly. We don't have much time."

Zeke followed the man out of the building. The guards lay sprawled beside the house, machete wounds all over their bodies. Three men dressed similar to his rescuer sat on their horses with two horses waiting for Zeke and the other man.

"Where is *La Rosa*?" Zeke asked.

"You will see," the man replied. "It will take us a few days to reach her. She is waiting for you. She will be happy you are still alive."

Zeke rode off with the men. His rescuer said Pauline would be happy to see him. He wasn't sure he would feel the same.

- 2 1 -

Pauline paced the meeting room as she chewed on her thumbnail. Antonio, Dominic and the others watched her, each keeping their thoughts to themselves. She'd been this way since she sent the Mambises to find and rescue Zeke, which was three days ago.

Dominic finally spoke up.

"I don't see why you are so nervous," he said. "This was your plan."

Pauline stopped pacing. She glared at Dominic.

Dominic held up his hands then backed away.

"I've had enough of this," Antonio said. "Whether we rescue your boyfriend or not isn't part of my plan. I'm gathering my men for the march east."

Pauline waved her hand absently. "Good luck to you, Antonio."

Antonio smiled. "Luck has nothing to do with it."

Antonio and Quintin left the room. Pauline continued to pace.

"I'm tired of this as well," Dominic said. "I'll check our supplies to make sure we're ready."

He strode for the door, but then stopped and placed his hand on Pauline's shoulder.

"We've waited long enough, *hermana*," he said. "It's time we begin our mission."

Pauline brushed his hand away. Dominic shrugged then left the room.

Pauline sat down then rocked back and forth, hugging herself as she rocked. *Zeke isn't supposed to be here but what did I expect*, she thought. A smile creased her face; Zeke was a bounty hunter and the woman he loved was missing. The smile faded. Did he love her? They lived together for years but not once had he told her so. But neither had she told him. It was a comfortable relationship and the two of them enjoyed it despite the whispers of the neighbors and congregation and the pastor's constant private lectures of them living in sin.

She stood and began pacing again. Of course, he loved her. He'd come all the way from Freedonia to rescue her, as if she needed to be rescued. But Zeke didn't know her past. She shook her head; he would have come for her anyway even if he did, or so she hoped.

Her worried musing was interrupted by a loud commotion outside the room. Dominic was the first to enter, a smirk on his face. He was followed moments later by two Mambises. Standing between them supported on their shoulders was Zeke. He was dirty, he stank, but at that moment he could not have looked more wonderful to her because above all else, he was alive. Pauline rushed to him, hugging him tight.

"Ouch," he said.

Pauline loosened her grip as she pulled away. She looked into Zeke's eyes as was disturbed by what she saw. He barely smiled and his eyes seemed more curious than joyful.

"Hey, Pauline," he said.

"Hello Zeke," she said. "I'm so happy you're safe."

Zeke nodded as his smile faded.

"I could use some food and a good bath if that's possible," he said. "Some new clothes, too."

"Of course," Pauline said. She looked at the Mambises.

"See to it," she said.

The men carried Zeke out of the room. Dominic came to her side, a frown on his face.

"This is the man who loves you?" he asked. "It looks to me you might be mistaken."

"If he didn't love me, then why would he come all this way?" Pauline said. There was bitterness in her voice.

"I think we should go now," he said. "The Freedonians are waiting."

"The Freedonians can wait a little longer," Pauline replied. "I need to make sure Zeke is taken care of."

"I'm not sure he wants your attention," Dominic said.

"You don't know what he wants," she replied.

Pauline walked out of the room. She found Antonio's soldiers standing guard outside the large master bedroom of the hacienda. They nodded as she entered. The room had its own bathroom in which Zeke bathed. A table filled with fruit was set just outside. She could here Zeke splashing about in the tub and for a moment was tempted to enter the bathroom and join him. But would he want her to?

Instead she sat in the chair nearby the table and waited. The door finally opened and Zeke emerged naked, drying his body with a towel. Pauline stood, taking him in with her eyes. Zeke looked up at her and his cool look stifled her roiling emotions. He said nothing as he dressed into the clothes set out for him. It was a Mambi uniform, the only clothes available in the makeshift barracks.

"Fits pretty good," Zeke said. He looked up at Pauline and shared a weak smile.

"You've been here almost an hour and you haven't kissed me once," Pauline said playfully.

"I'm not sure who I'd be kissing," Zeke replied. "Is it Pauline Rose or Paulina de Rosa?"

Pauline collapsed in the chair. "I should have told you."

Zeke sat on the bed. "Tell me now."

Pauline took a deep breath. "Twelve years ago, enslaved Cubans and Cuban planters had enough of New Spain's rule. Enslaved Cubans simply wanted to be free; the planters were tired of New Spain's harsh rule and heavy taxes. Both knew they could not be successful without each other so they decided to unite against the common enemy. Many Black Cubans had already escaped slavery and were fighting a small but intense war against the planters and New Spain. The planters met secretly with them and vowed to end slavery and immediately free any enslaved Cuban if they help support the revolution. The Black Cubans would not agree unless all enslaved Cubans were made free immediately, whether choosing to fight or not. An agreement was struck and the revolution began. But as the war continued and the planters began losing their wealth, they began to doubt the revolution. They met secretly with New Spain, agreeing to end the revolt for better representation. New Spain agreed to allow those Black Cubans who fought with the rebels to remain free, but to reinstate slavery to those who had not. In addition, all the military leaders of the revolution had to leave Cuba. I was one of those leaders."

"You were a slave?" Zeke asked.

"No," Pauline replied. "My mother, Angelica, was a seamstress in Havana. Her parents, my grandparents, had once been slaves. My father, Tomas, owned a sugar plantation. He met my mother through his wife. They had an affair, and I was the result."

Pauline hesitated as memories of her mother came to mind. "Mama was a beautiful soul. So kind and giving. I always wondered what she saw in my father and why she fell in love with him. They were so different."

A tear escaped her eye and she quickly wiped it away.

"My mother was always helping escaped Cubans and those newly emancipated. She gave clothes and even money when she could. She taught me how to care for and fight for those less fortunate. So, when the revolution began my mother and I volunteered. We moved to the countryside, hiding from the Spanish and doing what we could."

"What happened to your mother?" Zeke asked.

"She was killed in an ambush on our camp," Pauline replied. "It was that day that I became a fighter."

"Looks like you were pretty good at it," Zeke commented.

"I had a great teacher. I served under Antonio Maceo, 'The Bronze Titan.' Antonio brought the best out of all of us. We were winning the war until the Spanish planted the rumor that Antonio would make Cuba a Black nation like New Haiti if we won. We began losing the support of the planters then. Soon afterwards they met with the New Spanish authorities and signed the truce."

Zeke frowned. "You could have kept on fighting without them like you did before."

"We didn't have the money," Pauline said. "Besides, the planters turned on us, helping the Spanish authorities find us. That's why I left Cuba and came to Freedonia."

"Were you ever going to tell me?"

"Yes. No. I don't know. When I came to Freedonia my plan was to forget Cuba. I came to start a new life with Antonio. He was my only link to home, and when he died, I was committed to starting over . . . with you. But then your government decided they had a better use for me, and now we're here."

"Bastards," Zeke said.

Pauline reached out and grasped Zeke's hands.

"I can understand you being upset," she said. "But you came all this way to find me, which means you care about me as much as I care about you."

Zeke slipped his hands free of Pauline's.

"I came here for answers," Zeke said. "And I came here because nobody should be forced to do something they don't want to do. But I'm not sure I know you anymore. I see all this and I can't help thinking there might be something else you're hiding from me. I'm not the best man when it comes to a lot of things, but one thing I am is honest. I don't hold no secrets, especially from people I . . . I care about. I expect the same from them."

"Zeke, I . . ."

Dominic entered the room. He stared at Zeke a moment before addressing Pauline.

"We must go," he said. "If we wait any longer, we'll miss our rendezvous."

Pauline stood. "I have to go. I hope you'll stay here until I return."

Zeke stood as well. "I'm going with you."

"You can't. You need to rest."

"How do you expect me to rest when I don't have any idea where you're going or if you're coming back? No, I'm going."

Dominic folded his arms across his chest.

"This is a dangerous mission," he said.

Zeke grinned. "I'm a dangerous man."

Dominic glanced toward Pauline and she nodded.

"Zeke is a bounty hunter," she said.

"The best," Zeke added.

Pauline smiled, encouraged by his mood.

"He served in the Haitian army for a time and fought for Freedonia during the Reunion War," she continued. "He can handle himself."

"Welcome Zeke," Dominic said. "Now hurry. We must go."

As soon as Dominic left the room Pauline noticed Zeke's mood change.

"When we return, we can talk more," she said.

"If we return," Zeke replied.

- 2 2 -

Cuba burned with the flames of revolution. Antonio Maceo, the Bronze Titan, had returned and brought with him the fervor of freedom. Even the planters were inspired, although they still did not lend their full support to the new revolution. Their money remained in their hands, but they looked the other way as their slaves and workers slipped away in the darkness to support the insurgency. For some it was for change; for others it was to prevent becoming a victim of Maceo's scorched earth policy against those who supported New Spain. He and his Mambises ravaged *Occidente* Cuba, the local army and Spanish forces fruitless in their attempts to capture and defeat him. The image of Maceo and his Mambises charging from the forest mounted on their horses and waving their machetes haunted their enemies' sleep.

Far away from the fighting a small group of men and women waited in the forest bordering an unnamed harbor. Pauline gazed out into the horizon, her thoughts jumbled. There was a mission to complete, a task that would help the revolution and free her of her obligation to the Freedonians. And then there was Zeke, still distant. She had no time for emotions, but she couldn't help but worry about him. She had held back so much from him, things she thought she'd never have to share, things she realized she wanted to forget. But now all of it had surged up from the grave in which she buried it because of the selfish demands of a young nation.

A brief flash of light announced the arrival of their transportation.

"Get ready," she said to the others. "They're coming."

The rebels checked their gear. There were twenty in all, including Zeke. It seemed a small group for the task at hand, but the Mambises were used to long odds. Never had they gone into battle with the advantage; they had always been outnumbered and ill-equipped. They won because of their skill and passion, qualities their Spanish adversaries were hard pressed to match despite their numerical and technical superiority. The presence of the Freedonians would change the game, or so they promised. But first the Cubans had to find and destroy the mysterious ship.

The small steam boats came ashore making barely a sound. Pauline and the others climbed aboard without hesitation; Pauline noticed that Zeke climbed in the other boat. She broke her attention away and turned it to the Freedonian pilot.

"You know our destination?" she asked.

The Freedonian nodded. "The Isle of Pines."

"You can trust them," Dominic said. "There will be others waiting for us on the island."

Pauline stepped away from Dominic, anger welling in her chest.

"Others?"

"Calm down," he said. "They have . . . items that will help us on our mission."

"They are under my command or this mission is finished," Pauline said.

"Of course," Dominic replied.

The Freedonian hesitated, his eyes shifting between the two as he waited for orders. Pauline finally looked at the man.

"Take us," she said.

The pilot nodded then steered the boat back toward open water. Pauline worked her way closer to Dominic then grabbed his arm, digging her fingernails into his skin.

"Are there any other secrets you're keeping from me?" she asked.

"No,*La Rosa*," he replied. "The only other secrets are those that lie in the Spanish base."

Pauline's eyes narrowed as she studied Dominic. He was in the Freedonian's pockets deeper than she suspected. When this mission was over, he would probably disappear but it didn't matter. After this mission she would be done as well.

As her anger waned her curiosity took over. She worked her way to the back of the boat then stood beside the pilot.

"What makes the engine so silent?" she asked.

"Sound muffling technology developed at the Institute," he replied.

Pauline looked perplexed. "The Institute?"

The boatman smiled. "Tuskegee Institute. They create some amazing things there. GWC is a genius."

"GWC? Ah, George Washington Carver!"

The boatman nodded. "The one and only."

"Any other revelations I need to be prepared for?" she asked.

The boatman grinned. "I'm not privileged to tell, ma'am. You'll have to wait and see."

The boats cruised across the narrow channel to the island. They worked along the mangrove studded coast until they reached a small cove. A section of the cove had been cleared for landing. Five figures stood in the clearing, two of the-marmed, the other three with large packs strapped to their backs. The Mambises climbed over the boats' sides and into the shallow water. They waded to the shore, their weapons held over their heads. The two armed men smiled as they met Pauline and Dominic. The men were Cuban; the others with the back packs were Freedonian.

"*La Rosa*," the shorter of the two men said. "It is an honor to meet you. I have heard so much about you. I am Hernando Gomez. This is my comrade Juan Rodriguez."

Pauline shook the men's hands.

"It is good to have you as part of the revolution," she said. "Who are the others?"

The Freedonians approached, accompanied by Zeke. The first man to reach her, a tall athletically built fellow with ecru toned skin extended his hand.

"Hello Miss Rose. I'm Captain Adam Swan of the Freedonian Marines. This is Corporal Mitchell Gaines and Private William Hastings. We are here to help you destroy the ship."

"Welcome, Captain, Corporal, Private," Pauline said. "I assume your 'help' is strapped to your backs?"

The Captain grinned. "Yes, it is, ma'am."

Gomez interrupted their conversation.

"If everyone will follow me please," he said.

They trailed Gomez and the others to a small house a mile inland. Inside the structure were a single table and a kerosene lamp. Gomez lit the lamp then took a leather tube from under his shirt. He took out two maps, placed them on the table, unrolling them as everyone drew closer. Pauline was fascinated.

"What type of maps are these?" she asked.

"Aerial maps," Gomez replied. "Another gift from the Freedonians."

A closer look revealed the maps to be identical. Gomez superimposed the maps then took a case out of his pocket. He opened the case, revealing a black rectangle with two lenses supported by a wire stand. When he placed the lenses over the map, the overlapping areas transformed from flat to three dimensional, revealing the contours the landscape.

"When we first came to the island after receiving your information, we were very skeptical," Gomez said. "There was nothing indicating a shipyard unless it was hidden in the prison. We didn't have time to survey the entire island, so the Freedonians did high altitude flyovers and photographed every inch of it. When we studied the maps we discovered this."

Gomez pointed to a rise near the western coast of the island.

"That's too perfectly shaped to be natural," Pauline said. "They built the shipyard then disguised it as a hill."

Gomez nodded.

"So, we're not hitting the prison?" Dominic asked.

"No," Gomez said. "This is our target."

"We must strike both," Pauline replied.

"We're not here to liberate prisoners," Gomez said. "We're here to destroy a ship."

"We're here to do whatever we want to do," Pauline said. "You may have the technology, but we supply the manpower and we're not risking our lives just to blow up a ship if we cannot save our comrades."

Gomez and Pauline stared at each other for a moment before Gomez smiled.

"We will do as you say, as long as we strike the shipyard first."

"Of course," Pauline replied. "If the strike is successful it will provide a diversion."

"We are not obligated to help you attack the prison," Gomez said. "Our mission is the ship."

"I understand," Pauline replied. "We could use your help but it is not necessary. However, if you are true Cubans you would help without hesitation."

Gomez's eyes narrowed as his hands formed fists. Pauline straightened; Dominic and Zeke came to her side.

"There's no need for this," Captain Swan said. "Ma'am, the Freedonian Marines are at your service."

Pauline grinned. "Good. Now let's get moving. Gomez, lead the way."

Gomez rolled up the maps thenput them into the map holder. The team exited the house then made their way to the false hill. The terrain of the Isle of Pines was difficult; there were many small marshes and other obstacles which slowed the team down. As the crest of the hill broke the horizon the sky brightened in the east. Pauline was hoping for darkness;that was not to be.

"How do we get in?" Dominic answered.

Gomez frowned. "That I don't know *amigo.*"

"Spread out and search the perimeter," Pauline said. "The entrance is most likely concealed. If you find it do not enter. Signal the person closest to you then pass it along."

The team did as they were ordered. As they began to disperse Pauline called out.

"Zeke, you're with me."

Zeke turned slowly. He nodded his head then strolled up to her.

"Whatever you say, *La Rosa.*"

The sarcasm in his voice distracted her for a moment. Her face tightened.

"Stay focused," she said. "Can I depend on you?"

"Of course you can," Zeke said. "You know everything about me."

Pauline lowered her head to hide her anger. "Follow me."

Pauline and Zeke crept along the hill base, pressing their hands into the vines and brush as they sought for any irregularities that might indicate a way in. They were thirty minutes into their search when a runner came to them.

"*La Rosa,*" the woman said. "We found it!"

Pauline and Zeke followed the runner. The others were gathering as well. Dominic looked at her with a frown.

"It's a door, but it's designed to open from inside," he said.

"Can we force it?" she asked.

"Yes, but we don't know what's on the other side," he replied.

"That's why they're called dangerous missions," Zeke said.

He took his knife from his waist. As he ran his fingers along the door edge he dug into the slit with his knife, cutting away the vines.

"This one ain't been opened in a while," he said. "There are probably others."

"We should find them," Pauline said.

"No, this one will do," Zeke replied.

"What do you plan to do?" Gomez asked.

"What you always do when you want to get through a door," Zeke replied. "Knock."

Zeke kicked the door hard. Everyone else scattered, taking position on either side of the door.

"I thought you told me he was good," Dominic said.

"He is," Pauline replied. "A little reckless, too."

A voice came through the door.

"Jorge, es que usted?"

Zeke looked at the others then grinned before answering.

"Que?"

The door opened and a man with a bearded face stuck out his head. Zeke punched him across the jaw then caught him before he hit the ground. He dragged him aside; Pauline rushed to him then caught the door before it closed.

"Gag him and tie him up," Pauline said.

Dominic and Zeke bound the hapless guard in seconds. The others pulled their weapons and entered the false hill. The innards of the building were impressive. Metal supports rose from the ground then across the space for over five hundred yards before descending to the opposite side. Spanish sailors and soldiers crowded the docks, busy with their various tasks. There was only one problem; there was no ship.

Pauline glared at Gomez.

"What the hell is going on here?"

Gomez reached into his pocket then pulled out his watch.

"It's late," he said. "We were told it would have arrived by now."

"How can you know when this ship was supposed to arrive if it's such a big secret?" Pauline asked.

"La Rosa, let me explain . . ." Gomez began. He was cut off by blaring horns.

"We've been discovered!" Dominic shouted.

"Not quite," Zeke replied. "Look."

The Spaniards gathered around the empty docks with ropes in their calloused hands as the horns continued to sound in sequence. Moments later there was a disturbance in the water that grew into a rising mound of roiling water. The mysterious geyser fell away to reveal a metal spire. As the water receded an object took its place.

"I'll be damned," Zeke said.

"¡Madre mia!" Dominic said.

"A submersible," Pauline said.

The super ship continued to emerge. The concept of a submersible was not new; the Freedonians and other countries had developed them long ago. Never had there been a ship of this size capable of submerging into the depths. The implications of New Spain possessomg such a weapon were ominous.

The Freedonian Marines came forward.

"We need to get closer," Captain Swan said. "Our surprise has limited range."

"Let's move then," Pauline said. "Dominic, you and the Mambises spread out. Take anyone down who gets in the way. Do it silently as long as you can. As soon as you seen that thing blow, head back to this door as fast as you can."

Dominic nodded. He circled his hand over his head then pointed in every direction. The Mambises took out their machetes then dispersed.

"Zeke, we're with Gomez and the Marines," she said.

"Yes ma'am," Zeke took out his shotgun.

"No shooting, at least not yet," Pauline said.

"I suspect we'll be shooting before we get near that thing," Zeke replied. "Just trying to be prepared."

Pauline rolled her eyes.

"Let's move," she said.

Pauline and her team hurried across the open expanse. She glanced about, tracking the others as they made their way across the facility. So far there were no confrontations. Once again, the Spaniards were overconfident. It was a trademark of their war against the Cubans and it would be their demise.

"How much closer do we need to be?" she said to the captain.

"A few more feet," he answered. "We're almost . . ."

"Alto! Alto!"

Shots rang out all around them. Pauline fell to the ground as she took her rifle from her shoulder. The Spaniards had apparently allowed them to come out into the open. She peered up and saw what she feared. Spanish troops were advancing from all sides. A siren sounded, coming from the direction of the ship. She looked toward the ship and saw three Diablos creeping toward them.

"We're trapped!" Private Hastings shouted.

"You just figuring that out?" Zeke said. He lay on his back while loading his shotgun. "What's the call, *La Rosa*?"

"Stop it with the *La Rosa*!" Pauline said. "We'll have to trust Dominic and the others to draw off the soldiers. Our objective is the ship."

"Those doohickeys coming for us might have something to say about that," Zeke replied.

"We can handle the Diablos," the captain said. "But it won't leave us with enough rounds to destroy the ship. Not out here."

"Tell us the whole truth," Pauline said.

"We call them Stingers," the captain said. "They are self-propelled explosives. One projectile is powerful enough to take out a Diablo, but we have just enough to take out the ship. I figure one Stinger for each Diablo, which will leave us three. The only way we can destroy the ship with three Stingers is to get inside and fire them into the fuel reserves."

"So basically, we have to get inside then blow ourselves up with the ship?" Zeke asked.

"Yes," the captain replied.

"I don't think there's enough money in the whole wide world to convince me to do that," Zeke said.

"We'll find another way," Pauline said. "Zeke, you cover our right flank. I got left. Captain, we'll get you to that ship."

The captain looked skeptical but nodded. "Yes ma'am."

The team sprinted for the vanguard of Diablos. The other members were holding their own and doing a good job of keeping the Spaniards away. Pauline shot down anyone who broke through; the booming reaching her ears from behind told her

Zeke was doing his part as well. She cursed herself for doubting him; Zeke would never let anyone down in a fight.

"Hold tight!" the captain shouted. The Marines took a knee and unpacked their weapons. As they were assembling the lethal tubes the Diablos opened fire. Pauline dove to the ground as the Gatling guns raked their position. She turned to the Marines; the private lay on his back, his eyes blank. The captain grimaced as well. Only the corporal was unhurt. Zeke was already crawling toward the men. The two of them met at the captain.

"This ain't good," Zeke said. He jumped up then fired at the exposed cockpit of the central Diablo, emptying his shotgun. The vehicle careened to the right, slamming into its nearest cohort. The two machines did an awkward dance then stalled. The other three continued to advance.

"Captain, what do we do?" Pauline asked.

The captain grimaced before answering.

"Corporal, assemble the stingers!"

The corporal pushed the dead private onto his stomach, opened his pack then took the metal tubes out. In seconds the weapon was assembled. The captain crawled over to them then took out a long bullet like object with flaps extending from its base. He handed it to Pauline.

"Put this in the back of the tube then get out of the way," he said.

Pauline took the object then tried to insert it in the tube.

"It won't fit!" she shouted.

"Push harder," the corporal replied.

Pauline shoved the object into the tube.

"Stand clear!" the corporal said.

Pauline rolled away. The corporal took aim then pressed the trigger.

"Catch this!" he shouted.

There was a loud swooshing sound. A flash burst from the rear of the tube and the projectile streaked for a Diablo, leaving a smoke trail in its wake. It struck one of the vehicles and a loud explosion followed. Fire enveloped the vehicle as black smoke blocked it from view.

"Give me another one!" the corporal shouted.

Pauline shoved another projectile into the tube and the corporal fired again, striking the burning vehicles and unleashing a larger explosion. Warning alarms filled the hidden dock as the Spaniards attempted to converge on their position. Dominic and his men held them off.

"We need to speed this up," Zeke shouted. "Looks like our target is about to say *adios*."

Water churned around the giant submersible as its sailors scrambled to untie the mooring ropes.

"Let's move!" Pauline shouted.

Pauline, Zeke, the captain and the corporal jumped to their feet then sprinted toward the ship. The sirens shrieked, drowning out the gunfire. Pauline looked to either side of her and was pleased by what she saw. Her team handled the guards and advanced toward the ship. Her joy was smashed when two Diablos rolled out of the smoke. One of the vehicles showed damaged; the other unscratched.

The corporal immediately fell to his knees then threw the rocket tube on his shoulder. The captain grabbed a projectile from the pack, grimacing as he jammed it into the tube.

"Clear!" the corporal shouted. He fired the rocket; the projectile sped toward the target. Everyone except Pauline and Zeke halted, bracing for impact. Instead the Diablos veered and the projectile streaked passed it. But it did find a target. The projectile slammed against the ship then exploded. Fire flashed and smoke spewed from the base of the submersible. The damage forced the vessel to halt its descent.

"Zeke!" Pauline shouted. "Let's get those things before they get us!"

The duo jumped to their feet then sprinted toward the distracted Diablos.

By the time the Diablos were in position to fire Pauline and Zeke lurked between them. Zeke formed a cup with his hands and Pauline ran toward him. As she stepped into his hands, he tossed her as hard as he could. She jumped onto the front of the lead Diablo, landing on the coverings. Zeke was too close for the gunner to train the Gatlings on him; the other Diablo couldn't use its guns on fear of damaging its cohort. The gunners extracted their handguns and fired. The attempt was short-lived as a hail of bullets from the Mambises forced the gunners to retreat into the Diablos.

Zeke holstered his shotgun and was about to climb onto the *Diablo* when he was tackled to the ground. He twisted around to stare into the face of a Spanish sailor raising a knife over his head. Zeke punched the man in the throat; the man dropped the knife and grabbed his damaged neck. Zeke rolled away then took out his shotgun again. The Diablos halted and the sailors swarmed around them, some trying to shoot him, others exchanging gunfire with the Mambises. They were too close to the Diablos for them to be effective. As Zeke joined the battle, a question popped in his head. Where was Pauline?

Pauline climbed up the *Diablo,* stopping periodically to keep from tumbling off the machine as it shifted about. She finally reached the spotter's perch and quickly dispatched the man with a shot from her revolver. She clambered into the machine then worked her way to the pilot and the other crew members. The driver held the steering will with one hand while yelling frantically into a device he held in the other.

"Send more sailors and train the ship guns on our position . . . yes, I know we'll be damaged as well but the ship must be saved! Stop arguing with me. Do it now!"

Pauline jumped into the cockpit. The driver looked at her, dropped the device and let go of the steering wheel. She raised her revolver but one of the crewmen kicked it out of her hand then followed with another kick that hit her stomach and sent her tumbling back toward the edge of the cockpit. The crewman went low toward Pauline's legs. She braced the cockpit railing with both hands, pulled her knees to her chest then kicked both feet into his chest. The man careened across the cockpit, slamming into the others. Pauline pulled her machete free then fell upon the tangle of men, dispatching them quickly. After a brief inspection of her grim work she exited the Diablo innards, climbing back into the spotter's nest.

She peered over the edge and saw Zeke in the midst of the fray, swinging his machete with lethal effect.

"Zeke!" she shouted.

Zeke looked up and it almost cost him his life. A Spaniard charging him with his bayoneted rifle decided to shout his obvious victory; Zeke sidestepped his thrust then took off his head with a hard swing of his machete. He immediately sheathed the blade, grabbed his shotgun then climbed the Diablo. Pauline led him into the Diablo past her carnage then to the gunner's chair. A smile came to his face as he sat.

"I'll drive. You shoot," Pauline said.

Pauline swiveled the vehicle around to the remaining Diablo and Zeke opened fire, taking it out with a torrent of lead. She steered the vehicle about and accelerated toward the warship, Zeke shooting the sailors on the ground and those on the ship deck. They were pushing the Spaniards back when Pauline spotted the ship's massive gun turrets pivoting toward the group.

"*La Rosa*!" Zeke shouted. "I think you need to either get up closer to that boat or get us the hell out of here!"

Pauline pressed her foot on the accelerator and turned the steering wheel, hoping to get the *Diablo*out of the line of fire. Mambises scattered in every direction, running hard to avoid the firestorm the huge guns were about to unleash.

"Come on, come on!" Pauline said between her teeth.

The ship guns fired. A large explosion bloomed before the Diablo and it rose into the air. Pauline gripped the steering wheel as the vehicle flipped then landed hard. Her head struck the back plate; she blacked out briefly then awoke with a sharp pain on the back of her head. Miraculously the vehicle righted on its tracks.

"You okay?" she heard Zeke ask. He managed to stay in his seat, but his forehead was bruised and bleeding.

"No," Pauline answered.

"Good. Now get this damn thing moving before those turrets fire on us again!"

Another blast cut their conversation short; Pauline braced herself for the shock. It didn't come. More blasts rumbled above the Diablo like a coming storm.

"What the hell is going on?" Zeke asked.

Pauline looked overhead and saw a gaping hole rimmed by fire in the canopy, exposing the dawn sky. Moments later a Dragonfly flew through the hole into the secret hangar. Pauline laughed.

"The Freedonians are officially here," she said.

She watched the Dragonfly circle the area once then dive at the warship, its nose guns blazing. Sailors on deck scattered in every direction seeking cover. The aircraft then veered toward them, strafing the Spanish sailors. As the Dragonfly turned back toward the warship three more aircraft plunged through the gap. They were larger and slower craft, each with a large object attached to their fuselages.

"What are those?" she said

"Grasshoppers," Zeke answered. "I ain't never seen ones like these though."

The Grasshoppers released the objects as they jerked upward. The objects slammed into the warship; seconds later the submersible shook with three tremendous explosions. The aircraft climbed out of the hangar, followed by the Dragonfly. The warship continued to explode, the bombs apparently striking ammunitions and fuel.

"Let's get out of here," Pauline said.

She steered the *Diablo* toward their secret entrance. Dominic and another Mambises had commandeered the other Diablo and joined them.

Together they blew a wider hole into the hidden hangar then drove out, followed by their men. After they were clear of the hangar, Pauline stopped her *Diablo* and climbed down. She sought out and found Captain Swan. His wounds had been treated but he still bled.

"Captain, explain," Pauline said.

The captain half smiled and half grimaced.

"We had a backup plan," he said. "In the event we found the warship and wasn't able to destroy it we had a squadron in the vicinity prepared to finish the job. I telegraphed them after our bombs were spent."

Gomez frowned. "Freedonians."

The captain's eyes narrowed as he looked at Gomez.

"This was supposed to be a domestic incident," the captain said. "Now it's an international one. If your revolt is not successful Freedonia will be accused of attacking a nation with which it has diplomatic relations. There will be serious repercussions. But we believe in you and your cause. The world believes Cuba will become another Haiti, which is why they oppose your revolution. Even Haiti won't support you. You have to win this war now, for your sake and ours."

"He's right," Pauline said.

"Spoken like one of Tubman's boys," Zeke said. The captain grinned, confirming Zeke's suspicions.

"I'm not concerned about politics," Pauline said. "We have a prison to liberate. Captain, since they're already here, can we expect help from your aircraft?"

"Of course, ma'am," the captain replied.

"Then let's move," Pauline ordered.

The taking of the prison was a simple task compared to the warship hangar. The guards quickly surrendered when the Dragonflies and captured Diablos appeared. One strafing run and a round from the Diablos guns was all it took. The guards opened the gates and the Mambises rushed in. The prisoners were liberated and the guards and sailors from the hangar took their place.

Pauline and her team gathered in the warden's office. She was proud of each and every one of them and made it plain as she hugged them one at a time. She hesitated when she hugged Zeke; his reaction was reserved.

"We have to get back to the mainland," she said. "General Maceo needs us."

Once again, she turned to the captain. "Can you make it happen?"

"We have boats waiting for you," he said. "Although we won't be accompanying you."

"Understood."

"We could use a couple of those rocket tubes you got there," Zeke said. "They blow things up good."

The room echoed with laughter.

"I wish I could oblige, but that would be an obvious sign of Freedonian involvement," the captain said.

"I think those Dragonflies kind of did that for you," Zeke said.

The captain grinned. "I'll make you a promise. When you win this revolution, I'll personally deliver a boatload."

"I'm going to hold you to that promise," Pauline said.

Pauline filled her glass with rum then raised it high. The others repeated her gesture.

"*Viva la Cuba*!" she shouted.

"*Viva la Cuba*!" the others repeated.

As she tossed back her head to drink, her eyes found Zeke's. He gave her a slight smile then looked away.

- 2 3 -

The feast was almost ready. The smell of *moros y cristianos, chilindron de carnero* and strong *café* filled the air, making the hundreds of mouths waiting water in anticipation. The aromas drifted into the window of the room where Pauline dressed, her mind vacillating between so many emotions. The raid had been successful with little loss of life, which gave her a sense of satisfaction. Her good mood did not fare well against the other things that occupied her thoughts. She did not expect the death of her father to affect her as much as it did. She wasn't able to attend his funeral for she knew Gonzales would have his men waiting for her. Those that did told her it was an elaborate affair fitting a man of his status. She would visit and place flowers on his gravewhen the war was over.If not for herself, for her mother.

And then there was Zeke. He held his own during the raid, fighting by her side without hesitation. Yet afterwards he became distant again, keeping their conversations short and their contact minimum. She'd shared everything she could, but he still stayed away.

Drumming cut her musing short; the rumba had begun. She wrapped her scarf around her shoulders then inspected herself again before leaving the room. She felt a little silly; here she was the leader of a revolution and she had intentionally dressed to capture the attention of a man.

"La Rosa, what is wrong with you?" she said.

When Pauline emerged from her room Dominic waited for her.

"This is a surprise," she said.

"I wanted to congratulate you for the mission's success," he said. "I also wanted to be the first to dance with you tonight. I'm glad that I came here. You look beautiful."

"Thank you," she said. "Where is Zeke?"

Her question diminished Dominic's smile.

"Your Freedonian is entertaining the elders with his stories," he said. "He seems quite sociable."

"He can be," Pauline said.

The two strolled out of the museum and into the warm night. The celebration took place in Matanzas square. Pauline searched the crowd for Zeke and found him sitting under a large tree with the elders. He gestured as he spoke, the listeners caught up in his story.

"I was wrong about you," Dominic said.

"What?" Pauline pulled her attention from Zeke.

"I thought you wouldn't be focused enough on the situation in Cuba to be of use to us," he said. "I said as much to the elders and the Freedonians before you arrived."

"Thank you for your confidence," she replied. "If you are trying to get me to like you, you're doing a terrible job."

"I'm being honest," Dominic replied. "After this is all over, I would like to get to know you better."

"After this is done, I'm returning to Freedonia," Pauline replied.

"I don't think so," Dominic said. "You love Cuba too much, and I don't think there is anything for you there anymore."

She glared at Dominic.

"Goodbye."

She stalked away, headed for Zeke and the elders. Zeke saw her approaching and his voice faded. He stood and nodded to her.

"Pauline," he said.

She grabbed his hand then led him away, walking until she found a secluded place. Then she turned around and kissed him. His lips were tense against hers but then yielded. She felt his arms slide around her waist then pull her tighter against him. It was a long, deep kiss that still ended to soon.

"I missed you so much," she said.

"I missed you, too. But Pauline . . ."

She pressed her fingers against his lips.

"Not today Zeke, please," she asked. "Let's just imagine us before all this."

"Hear me out," he replied. "My life ain't been the easiest, or the most comfortable. I can count the number of times I've been in love with one hand with four fingers missing. The fact is I can jump into the toughest fight you can imagine without a second thought. But this right here scares me, because when it when it hurts it hurts deep and it lasts long. Sometimes the pain never goes away."

Pauline looked into Zeke's eyes and felt shame.

"If I could do it over again, I'd tell you everything," she said. "But I can't. I can tell you that I would never hurt you again and that your heart is safe with me."

She kissed him again then grasped his hand.
"Come with me," she said.
"Pauline, I don't think . . ."
"Don't think. Just come with me."
Zeke relented. They walked hand in hand back to the museum and into her room.

- 2 4 -

Cuba was in turmoil once again. General Antonia Maceo continued his lighting raids throughout the Oriente. General Gomez had returned and taken command the rebel forces in the Occidente. Slave revolts plagued those planters still loyal to the Spanish-supported Cuban government and citizens throughout the island flocked to the rebel cause. Those planters that did not support the ruling government supplied the rebels with food and arms. The Freedonian and Haitian navies set up an unofficial blockade of the island; the supplies that slipped through to the Spanish forces were not enough to stem the rising resistance. Worse of all, word of the successful raid on the Isle of Pine and the destruction of the secret submersible finally reached New Spain's military council, ending all hopes of New Spain breaking Freedonia's dominance of the Caribbean Sea. The Spaniards suspected Freedonians were involved, but there were no reports from the island to confirm or deny their suspicions.

Gonzales pondered these things as he sat at the conference table in the governor's office. He was wasting his time with the governor and the American ambassador, but the governor insisted that he and his men be present. He gave many vague explanations as to why but the real cause, the reason he would not admit, was that he was afraid. To the Spanish coward it was bad enough to have La Rosa on the loose, but with both General Maceo and Gomez in Cuba as well it was beyond dangerous. All the more reason Gonzales should be in the field, not entertaining foreign diplomats.

Ambassador Wainwright puffed his cigar then took it from his mouth and grinned.

"Damn fine cigar," he said. "Excellent."

"Only the best from Cuba," the governor said. "Now, if we can discuss . . ."

The ambassador raised his hand. "Not quite yet, Governor. I'd like to savor this wonderful cigar a few more minutes before we get down to business."

Gonzales snarled as he leaned toward the ambassador in his seat. The governor glared at Gonzales and he sank back into his seat like a scolded guard dog. Give him five minutes with this pompous bastard and Cuba would be drowning with support from America, Gonzales thought. The governor insisted that torture was not an option, but Gonzales had ways of getting what he wanted without leaving any physical evidence while inflicting permanent mental damage. It was his specialty.

Wainwright wasted another ten minutes with his cigar before finally placing it down in the tray sitting on the stand beside his chair. He picked up his glass of rum, took a mouthful, swishing it around in his mouth before swallowing.

"Cuba is such a sensual place," he commented. "Now, Governor, what is it you want from America?"

"Your support," the governor said. "It is obvious to us that Freedonia is behind the uprising."

"I don't see how you drew that conclusion," Wainwright said, his eyes narrowing. "Didn't they give you the whereabouts of Paulina De Rosa? In our eyes Cuba and Freedonia are allies, which doesn't sit well with our government. Not well at all."

"It was a ruse," Gonzales said. "It was their way of getting her into the country."

"It worked," Wainwright said. "Which makes me question the astuteness of your people, governor."

That statement was meant for Gonzales. The general rose from his seat but a sharp shake of the governor's head forced him to return to his seat. He smiled at the insolent American as he imagined dragging him behind the governor's hacienda for serious negotiations.

"Be that as it may, the fact remains that we need your help," the governor said. "The Haitians and Freedonians have established a blockade in the Caribbean, turning back all shipments destined to Cuba. The only countries strong enough to challenge that blockade are the British, the French, and America."

Wainwright rubbed his beard. "The British have their own issues in Africa and Asia, and the French don't care at all. This leaves us."

The governor nodded. "Yes. You must understand the gravity of the situation, ambassador. If Cuba falls it is more than likely that Antonio Maceo will become its king."

Wainwright's aloofness dissipated on the mention of The Bronze Titan.

"I thought Maceo answered to Gomez."

"He does . . . for now," the governor said. "Maceo has no patience for politics, which is why he is such a threat. The planters believe in Gomez, but the army follows Maceo and La Rosa. If the rebels achieve victory the spoils will go to Maceo. If Maceo becomes ruler of Cuba, our country will become another Haiti."

Gonzales smiled when the governor mentioned Haiti. The fear of another Black republic in the Western Hemisphere was a rallying point for all involved.

"I'll see what I can do," Wainwright said. "You know you're asking for a declaration of war against Freedonia."

"It was inevitable," the governor said. "Certain elements of your population have been urging for such an action for quite some time."

"How did you know that?" the ambassador asked.

The governor grinned. "America isn't the only country with spies."

Wainwright's mouth opened to respond when two explosions shook the room. Gonzales was on his feet almost immediately. He sprinted to the front door of the hacienda, his revolver in his hand. When he opened the door he was greeted by the sound of heavy gunfire. He hurried back to the room; the governor and the ambassador looked at him with expectant faces.

"We're under attack," Gonzales said. "Mambises."

The Governor blanched. "The Mambises? How? Maceo and Gomez are hundreds of miles from here. How could they cover so much ground so quickly?"

Gonzales had to think only a moment before the answer came to him.

"It's neither one of them," he finally said. "It is *La Rosa*."

Gonzales couldn't imagine the governor getting any paler, but he did.

"We have to leave now!" Wainwright exclaimed.

"It's too late," Gonzales said. "We'd be cut down before we reached the tree line. Are there rifles in this house?"

"Yes," the governor replied.

"Can you handle them?" Gomez asked.

The governor nodded.

"I can, too," the ambassador said.

Gonzales looked at the man with renewed respect.

"Good. Go upstairs and arm yourselves."

Gonzales marched out the rear of the house where his horse and cavalry waited. Rafael Castile, the cavalry commander, eased his mount beside him.

"She came as you said she would," he said.

"Never underestimate the power of revenge," Gonzales replied. "Shall we greet her, *Amigo*?"

Rafael smiled. "Of course."

Gonzales spurred his horse and the riders followed him around the house. As he suspected the Mambises charged toward the house on their steeds, their machetes drawn. At the head of the formation was Paulina; beside her rode the Freedonian Zeke Culpepper. Gonzales knew well the devastating effect of those attacks and planned to meet it head on.

"Sabers!" he shouted. The Spanish cavaliers drew their sabers as they surged toward the Mambises. The Mambises veered toward the Spaniards without hesitation.

The two sides met in a thunderous clash of steel and horseflesh. Gonzales slashed the throat of the first Mambises to reach him, his eyes focused on Pauline. He battled his way toward her, his skillful swordplay no match for the inexperienced rebels. He grinned as his eyes met Paulina's; the ground between them clearing as if their meeting was inevitable.

Gonzales's saber crashed against Pauline's machete and the duo dueled furiously for an advantage. Gonzales's confidence transformed into frustration as Paulina thwarted his every thrust and slash despite the reach advantage of his saber. The woman was skilled beyond his expectations. He was beginning to question his decision to battle her this way. It was time to bring this game to an end.

As he reached for his revolver with his free hand Paulina did the unexpected; she jumped from her saddle, crashing into Gonzales. They both tumbled to the ground in a tangled heap. Gonzales felt a sharp pain in his left side as he struck the ground; he shoved Paulina from atop of him.

Gonzales reached out and found his saber hilt just in time to block the cleaving stroke from Paulina's machete. He managed to sweep her feet and she fell onto her back, giving him time to stand. His respite was brief; Paulina pounced with the fury of a wildcat. Gonzales's arms tired as Pauline hammered at him. In desperation he yelled and thrust his sword at her; a burning pain emitted from his right leg and he collapsed. He looked down; Paulina had severed it below the knee. As he fell more pain flashed from his left arm and then his right. A final excruciating blow from his left leg sent Gonzales into brief unconsciousness. When he recovered

Pauline stood over him, a sneer marring her beautiful face. He lay on his back limbless.

"Go ahead," he managed to say. "Finish it. Kill me."

Pauline's spit hit his face.

"You're already dead," she replied. She turned then walked away.

* * *

Pauline ignored Gonzales's desperate screams. She stalked toward the governor's hacienda where the Cuban militia and Spanish soldiers were making a final stand. A shotgun boomed and Pauline flinched. She turned to see Zeke standing over Gonzales's dead body. The look on his face was disapproving but she didn't care. That piece of trash had murdered Mary and her father. Better he suffered before entering whatever hell waited for him.

"Cease fire!" she shouted. The Mambises responded, lowering their guns. The trapped soldiers ceased as well. Pauline stood in the open, aware that she could be shot dead at any moment.

"Governor, we do not wish to kill you," she shouted. "My vengeance has been sated. All we ask is that you and your men surrender. You will be held as prisoners of war until we have won. Afterwards you will be free to live a peaceful life if you pledge loyalty to the new government. If that is not of your liking you can leave Cuba. The American ambassador is free to go as well."

The governor burst through the front door of the hacienda, the American ambassador close behind.

"We surrender! We surrender!"

"Maria! Pauline shouted.

Maria, her second in command, emerged from the safety of a large oak tree.

"Take them into custody," Pauline said.

Maria nodded. She waved her hand as she marched to the hacienda and five Mambises followed her to the home. As they approached the remaining occupants walked out of the hacienda without their guns, their hands raised in surrender. The other Mambises stood, every one of them looking at Pauline. It was over. The governor was in custody. Soon she would send messengers to both Maceo and Gomez. The militia and the Spaniards were sure to lose their will to fight upon hearing of the governor's capture. The generals would secure both Occidente and Oriente.

She stabbed her machete into the air.

"*Viva la Cuba!*" she shouted.

"*Viva la Cuba!*" the Mambises repeated.

As she walked toward her warriors, she resisted the urge to turn toward Zeke. He was another matter for another time. For now, she would savor her victory. No, she would savor Cuba's victory.

- 25 -

Pauline strode down the wide hallway of the Palacio de los Capitanes Generales, seeking the office of General Antonio Maceo. The new leaders of Cuba occupied the spacious palace soon after the governor surrendered. The Spanish government vehemently protested the occupation and threatened an invasion to reclaim the island, but their threats were hollow. Freedonia and New Haiti recognized Cuban independence and the former rebels as the legitimate government. Alliance negotiations began soon afterwards, assuring that the combined fleets of both nations would not allow any Spanish intervention. The United States remained neutral on the issue, fearing a declaration of support for New Spain would spark a war on the continent for which it was ill-prepared. The status quo would remain for the foreseeable future.

Pauline found Maceo sitting at an elaborate desk in a sparse office, reading over one of many documents which required signing to finalize the transition.

"General Maceo, you sent for me?"

The general looked up and a smile came to his grizzled face.

"Yes, *La Rosa*, I did. Please sit."

Pauline sat in the solitary seat before the desk. Maceo leaned back in his chair, the smile still gracing his face. No one had fought harder and sacrificed more for the revolution.

"Paulina, I would first like to thank you for everything you've done. Without you, our revolution would not have been revived."

"I can't claim credit for that," she said. "It was Freedonian intrigue that brought me back. I doubt if I would have done so on my own."

"Still, your bravery and skill rekindled the revolution, for which the Cuban people are eternally grateful."

Maceo stood and began pacing.

"Our new government is in need of brave and intelligent people to lead it into the future. I was hoping that you would be one of those people."

Pauline jumped in surprise. "Me? General, I appreciate your confidence in me, but I'm just a soldier."

"I am too, Pauline. Yet I'm willing to sacrifice peaceful days ahead in order to help our new nation gain its footing."

Pauline's mind was in turmoil. This was an offer she never expected. She had planned to return to Freedonia, but this was an opportunity she found intriguing.

"I'll have to think on this, General," she finally said.

"I understand," Maceo replied. "But don't take too long. We have a nation to build."

Pauline left the Palicio in a daze. She hailed a steam taxi.

"The Freedonian Embassy, please."

"Si, senora."

She contemplated this new opportunity during the ride, her musing interrupted as the taxi jerked to a stop before the embassy. The guards recognized her and let her through. She hurried to the receptionist desk.The dark brown woman at the desk greeted her with a smile.

"How can I help you, Miss Rose?"

"I've come to see Ezekiel Culpepper."

"Mr. Culpepper is not here," the woman said.

"Where is he?" Pauline asked.

"He's at the harbor," the receptionist replied. "He's catching the next ship to Freedonia."

Pauline raced back to her taxi.

"The harbor. Now!"

The driver sped through the streets and reached the harbor in minutes. Pauline ran to the harbormaster.

"You have a ship leaving for Freedonia?" she asked.

"Yes, *La Rosa*," the harbormaster replied with a wide smile. "The *Princess*. It departs from Dock Seven. I can have someone take you there."

"*Gracias*," she said.

"*Nada*," the harbormaster replied. The harbormaster led Pauline to a young man sitting in a jitney.

"Pablo, take *La Rosa* to Dock Seven immediately!"

Pablo saluted Pauline as she climbed into the back of the jitney. The young driver deftly maneuvered the jitney through loaders, workers and passengers until he reached Dock Seven. The passengers were proceeding up the gangplank. Pauline spotted Zeke; she jumped from the jitney and ran to the ship.

"Zeke! Zeke! Wait!"

Zeke looked about until he saw her. He worked his way through the other passengers. Pauline threw herself on him, hugging his neck tight. He did not hug her back. She let go of him, regaining her composure.

"You were going to leave without telling me?" she asked.

"I didn't see a reason to," Zeke replied. "Besides, I figured you would be busy."

Pauline reached down, gathering his hands into hers. "Zeke, I understand how you feel. You didn't know about this part of my life. I should have told you and I'm sorry. But I can't believe you're just going to give up on us. You came this far to find me."

"The woman I was looking for was not the woman I found," Zeke replied. "Truth is I don't know who you are at all. I don't know how much of the woman I fell in love with was real and how much of her was a lie."

"Do we really know everything about anyone?" Pauline asked.

Zeke pulled his hands away from Pauline's then raised his arms wide as he turned around as if on display.

"This is me," he said. "I never held any secrets from you. I've been honest every step of the way, good and bad."

"So now you know who I am," Pauline said. "Stay here. Please."

"I can't," Zeke said. "I need to be home to sort things out. You could come with me."

Pauline couldn't answer. There was so much work to do in Cuba, so much she was responsible for.

Zeke shook his head. "I thought so. Goodbye Pauline. I wish you well."

Pauline reached out and touched Zeke's cheek.

"Goodbye, *mi amor*," she said, her voice almost a whisper.

Zeke turned away then walked up the gangplank, disappearing into the throng. Pauline stood at the dock as the workers removed the gangplank then untied the ship. She watched as it eased from the dock then set out into the harbor. She did not move until the ship had disappeared over the horizon.

EPILOGUE

The ornate carriage rolled down the Havana streets, passing by building after building flying the flag of a free Cuba. The women inside the carriage smiled with pride, for they had been instrumental in its liberation and in forming the new government that rose in the wake of New Spain's capitulation. The people voted Gomez as president after Antonio Maceo, true to his word, refused to accept the position. The Bronze Titan was vigorous in his efforts to establish a free and equal Cuba, but no sooner had he done so did he begin to lobby for a revolution in Puerto Rico.

Pauline peered from the window, her face and mind filled with satisfaction. After twelve years the dream had been realized. She looked across the cabin to Alejandra and they both smiled.

"Are you sure you want to do this?" Alejandra asked.

"I've had two years to think about it," Pauline replied. "I'm sure."

Alejandra's face drooped. "I'm losing my sister again!"

Pauline reached out to touch Alejandra's cheek."

"Not like before, *hermana*. This time I'll be back much sooner."

"To stay or to visit?"

Pauline looked pensive. "I don't know."

The carriage took the ladies to Havana Harbor where the Freedonian steamship *F.S. Liberation* waited. Freedonia was the first nation to recognize Cuban sovereignty. President Douglass visited the island a year after the end of hostilities and signed a cooperative agreement, promising to provide financial and military support to the new nation. New Haiti's recognition soon followed. The European nations were slow to accept, and New Spain refused. They still considered the island a colony in revolt even though they were in no position to challenge its sovereignty.

Pauline and Alejandra strolled to the gangplank of the ship. They exchanged hugs and kisses before Pauline boarded.

"He doesn't deserve you," Alejandra said.

"Maybe I don't deserve him," Pauline replied.

"If it doesn't work out, come home quickly," Alejandra said. "I'll find you a handsome Cuban man who smokes cigars and will sing you love songs as he kisses your thighs."

They shared a laugh then hugged again.

"Adios, *hermana*," Pauline said.

"*Adios, Rosa dulce*," Alejandra replied.

Pauline waved as she walked up the gangplank. She reserved a first-class cabin for the trip, a luxury she rarely afforded herself but Alejandra insisted that she accept as a gift. The porters brought her bags to her room. She didn't know what to pack because she had no idea how long she would be gone. She settled into her surroundings, reading a book for a time before taking a long-deserved nap. When she woke, she changed into her evening wear then made her way to the ship's dining hall. The waiter sat her at her table then brought her a cup of tea. She was studying the menu when she saw someone approach from the corner of her eye.

"Excuse me, *senorita de Rosa*. May I sit?"

Pauline looked up to a familiar face and smirked. The man was dressed much differently than the last time she saw him, the suit and derby fitting his fit frame snugly. He took off his hat then bowed.

"Captain Swan," she said. "Fancy meeting you here."

"It's just Adam Swan now," he said. "You can call me Adam. Soldiers that fight together are comrades forever."

"Please, sit," she offered.

Adam pulled out the chair and sat.

"I don't think this is a coincidence," Pauline said.

"It's not."

A waiter appeared at the table.

"What would you like to drink, sir?"

"Nothing," Adam responded. "This is a short visit."

The waiter nodded then walked away.

"To what do I owe this visit?" Pauline asked.

"We're curious about your visit to Freedonia," Adam said.

"There's no need to worry. I don't plan on starting any revolutions."

Adam laughed. "That we know. We're wondering if your visit will be temporary or permanent."

"I can't answer that," she said. "That decision is not in my hands at the moment."

Adam looked at her knowingly. "I see."

"How is he?" Pauline asked.

"As well as can be expected," Adam answered. "We don't keep close tabs on him. But he's not our concern. I've been tasked to make you an offer, an offer which comes directly from Ms. Tubman."

"Really," Pauline said.

"We'd like you to work for us," Adam said. "You've more than proven your ability and it would do well for us to have someone close to the new Cuban government."

"You want me to spy on my own people," Pauline said.

"Yes," Adam replied.

Pauline laughed. "You're not one to sugar coat things, are you?"

"We're comrades. There should be no secrets between us."

Adam's words reminded her of Zeke and sobered her mood.

"I'll consider it," she said.

"That's all we ask."

Adam stood. "Of course, this offer remains between us."

"Of course," Pauline replied. "As you say, we are comrades."

"Enjoy your dinner," Adam said. "I hope all goes well for you in Freedonia."

Pauline's smile faded.

"I hope so, too."

The remainder of the voyage was uneventful. Pauline took advantage of the time, spending long days on deck reading and sharing small talk with the other passengers. They arrived in Savannah on a clear day, but Pauline's mood was just the opposite. The porters dropped her bags off on the dock as she waited for the only person she told of her visit. A small wagon driven by a large Black man rolled up to her. The man tipped his hat then smiled.

"Welcome back Miss Pauline," Big Pete said.

"Hello, Pete." Pauline climbed into the wagon then kissed Pete's cheek.

"Thank you so much for meeting me. I didn't think you would want to see me."

"Whatever happened back then wasn't your fault," he replied.

He loaded her bags into the wagon and they set off, stopping once for Pauline to purchase flowers. Two hours later they traveled down the dirt road leading to the Beulah AME Church cemetery. Two people waited for them under the shade of a live oak tree. As they came closer Pauline recognized Jeremiah and Bessie. Jeremiah wore a white shirt covered by overalls and a straw hat; Bessie looked cute in a short sundress decorated with flower print, a small bonnet pressed on her thick hair. They ran to the wagon, greeting Pauline with smiles and waves.

"Hey Miss Pauline!" Bessie exclaimed. "I thought I'd never see you again!"

Pauline climbed out the wagon and hugged the young woman. Jeremiah sauntered up to her and gave her a tight squeeze.

"Hi there, Miss Pauline. Sure is good to see you."

Bessie frowned. "Don't get too excited."

"I'm sorry, sugar. I didn't mean it that way."

Pauline's curious look was answered by Bessie lifting her hand to show a plain gold band around her finger.

"Me and Jeremiah is married!"

Pauline laughed. "Now that's a surprise."

"A surprise for me too," Jeremiah said. Bessie took a swing at Jeremiah and he leaned away.

"Pauline didn't come to see y'all fuss," Big Pete said. "She came to pay her respects."

Mama Mary's grave was only steps away. Pauline knelt before it, placing the flowers beside the simple headstone.

"Thank you," she whispered.

Bessie began to cry and Jeremiah hugged her close.

"She was like a mama to us," he said. "A mama to us all. But she's still with us in our hearts."

"Yes, she is," Pauline said.

Big Pete handed everyone handkerchiefs.

"I got supper at my house if anyone's hungry," he said. "We can eat and catch up on things. It's been a while."

"That sounds wonderful," Pauline said.

She spent the day with Jeremiah, Pete and Bessie. Afterwards Pete took her back to town and helped her find a decent hotel to spend the night. The next day she was up early to catch the first airship to Atlanta. She'd never been so nervous in her life.

* * *

Pauline watched Zeke pull back on the harness, stopping the old mule in its tracks. He looked behind himself and smiled. He'd done a good job, finishing the plowing in good time. At this rate he would finish both fields by the end of the week. He unharnessed the mule then led it back to the barn. She waited until he trudged back into the house before urging her horse on. As she neared Zeke re-emerged carrying a mason jar and a pitcher of sweet tea. He had settled into his rocking chair and was pouring a glass when he noticed her. She rode up to the hitching post then secured her horse. Zeke set his glass down then walked toward her, a smile growing on his face. When he reached her she extended her hand. He took it gently then shook it. She smirked as he let it go.

"Hello Ezekiel Culpepper," she said.

"Hello, ma'am," Zeke replied. "What brings you out this way?"

"I came to see an old friend," she replied. "I was hoping he would be happy to see me."

Zeke looked her up and down. "He might be. Does he know you?"

Pauline's smile faded. "No, he doesn't. But given time he will. And I believe he will love me more than he used to."

Zeke extended his arm and Pauline wrapped her hand around it.

"Let me show you my farm," he said. "We can talk along the way."

"I'd be delighted," she said.

They ambled toward the freshly plowed field.

"So, tell me about yourself," Zeke asked.

Pauline looked into his eyes and smiled. It seemed her visit would be longer than she anticipated.

"My name is Paulina de Rosa. I was born in Havana, Cuba . . ."

ABOUT THE AUTHOR

Milton Davis is an award winning Black Fantastic writer and owner of MVmedia, LLC, a publishing company specializing in Science Fiction, Fantasy and Sword and Soul. Milton is the author of twenty novels and editor/co-editor of seven anthologies. Milton's work had also been featured in *Black Power: The Superhero Anthology*; Skelos 2*: The Journal of Weird Fiction and Dark Fantasy Volume 2*, *Steampunk Writes Around the World* published by Luna Press and *Bass Reeves Frontier Marshal Volume Two*. Milton's story 'The Swarm' was nominated for the 2018 British Science Fiction Association Award for Short Fiction. His screenplay, Ngolo, won the 2014 Urban Action Showcase Award for Best Screenplay. Milton Davis can be reached via his website, https://www.miltonjdavis.com/

More Steamfunk Titles from MVmedia!
www.mvmediaatl.com

From Here to Timbuktu by Milton J. Davis

The year is 1870. As the young country of Freedonia prepares to celebrate fifty years of existence, a young bounty hunter by the name of Zeke Culpepper is hired by a wealthy businessman to find a valuable book. In the kingdom of Mali on the continent of Africa, veteran warrior Famara Keita has been assigned to find that same book and bring it back to its rightful owner. And in the newly formed nation of Germany, an ambitious Prussian officer seeks the book as well for its secrets that could make Germany the most powerful nation in the world. The result is an action adventure like no other!

Steamfunk! Edited by Balogun Ojetade and Milton J. Davis

A witch, more machine than human, judges the character of the wicked and hands out justice in a ravaged Chicago. John Henry wields his mighty hammers in a war against machines and the undead. Frederick Douglass and Harriet Tubman rule a country of freed slaves that rivals – and often bests – England and France in power and technology. You will find all this – and much more – between the pages of Steamfunk, an anthology of incredible stories by some of today's greatest authors of Science Fiction, Fantasy and Steamfunk – African and African American-inspired Steampunk.

Editors Milton Davis and Balogun Ojetade have put together a masterful work guaranteed to transport you to new worlds. Worlds of adventure; of terror; of war and wonder; of iron and steam. Open these pages and traverse the lumineferous aether to the world of Steamfunk!

Masquerade By Milton J. Davis

In the city of Barakoa, the mask is everything. It signifies your rank, your personality, your past, present and future. Jeremy Pepperdine waited for all these things to be bestowed upon him on his sixteenth birthday. But after a tragic event Jeremy finds himself, abandoned, alone....and maskless. How does a person survive in a world where the most important item of the society is denied to him?

CPSIA information can be obtained
at www.ICGtesting.com
Printed in the USA
FSHW011950270721
83618FS